ALSO BY JUSTIN COURTER

Skunk: A Love Story

The Death of the Poem and Other
Paragraphs

The Heart of It All

The Heart of It All

A Novel

Justin Courter

Owl Canyon Press

First Edition, 2014

All Rights Reserved

Library of Congress Cataloging-in-Publication Data

Courter, Justin.

The Heart of It All—1st ed.

p. cm.

ISBN: 978-0-9911211-1-3

2014935637

Owl Canyon Press

Boulder, Colorado

1

I got sick of it in the first few days—people telling me how terrible it is for Beatrice to be losing her memory. I don't see it like that. I mean, who wants to remember all this crap? She used to be in such control, they say, even taking care of Stanley at the end. Well maybe she never wanted control in the first place, I say. Maybe she wanted to forget. Then they look at me like, "Holy shit, dementia really is hereditary!"

Shouldn't Beatrice be allowed, though, to give up the steering wheel, figuratively speaking, after eighty-four years? Shouldn't she be allowed to say the hell with the whole highway if she wants? To get out of the car and wander around for a while?

That's actually why I came back to the Nasty—Cincinnasty, Ohio. My cousin Sheila told me how Beatrice had been walking through this devastated part of what used to be downtown and some friends of Maylene's happened to drive by. It was sunny out and Beatrice was carrying an umbrella, making her way along a sidewalk strewn with broken bottles. The couple slowed their car down and called out the window to Beatrice. She smiled and waved, but didn't seem to know who they were. They asked Beatrice where she was headed and she said Findlay Market. Which wasn't even open that day. They offered her a ride and drove her back to her farmhouse out forty-five miles east of the city. Beatrice couldn't tell them where her car was or if she'd taken it downtown.

Maylene was looking at this as an opportunity to lock her mother up in an overpriced prison, so when I heard about it I came back and moved in with Beatrice. Seems like ever since my parents died, Maylene's been trying to get rid of Beatrice too, like she's frustrated she can't finish tidying up, disposing of all her relatives. And that's why I came back. Not because of Carla.

The first thing I noticed, riding in on the bus, besides that I'd forgotten what a rinky-dink dump of a town this is, was all the billboards. I guess billboard proliferation is part of nature, but this was a Vegas number of billboards here in cow country. It got me kind of excited. I felt something like what I guess a painter feels when he has a fresh canvas in front of him.

I forgot about that, though, when I got off the bus and saw Carla standing in the middle of the terminal. She had her back to me, her weight on her right leg so her cute butt stuck out to the side. Her hand on her hip. Like she was waiting for me and getting impatient because I was late, as usual. My heart stopped beating. I even stopped walking and let the weight of my pack settle on my shoulders. Then my heart started beating way too fast. If it had been about five years before, I would have just gone over and looped my arm through the one propped on her hip. But it was now, not the '90s. So I stood there in the first year of this brave new millennium, paralyzed by the knot tying itself in my throat till all the sudden she turned around and looked right at me. And it was just like all the other times I'd seen her before in different cities all over the country. She was somebody else.

Well, what the hell were you thinking, you stupid idiot? I asked myself. That she somehow found out you were coming back and would be waiting around for you down here with all the bums and garbage and whatnot? Jesus Christ, snap out of it!

Now it's been two weeks and here I lurk—in a place from the past that I hadn't planned to come back to anytime soon (not that I had a plan at all, and it's a relief to have a free place to stay)—with what are starting to smell a whole lot like responsibilities. So I've got other stuff besides Carla to think about. Like where I'm supposed to take Beatrice today. I really don't need Maylene to come and remind me. Beatrice and I are sitting on the porch, just enjoying the cool early spring morning. It rained all yesterday, rinsing the world, which looks brand new with beads of water all over everything, glinting in the early slanting sunlight. It's so clear you can practically see the veins in each individual leaf that has begun to un-scroll itself from the maple near the porch. And here comes Maylene bombing down the driveway in her gold-embroidered SUV. When she gets out and climbs down from the vehicle, there's an angry tension in her tendons. She comes stalking up the walkway all wobbly because of the spike heels that are like two exclamation points her whole rigid frame is balanced on. Beatrice shifts around in her chair, uncomfortable already. Now Maylene is pulling her sunglasses down her nose and looking at us over the top of them as her heels knock and stutter on the flagstones. She mounts the porch and stands in front of us with her legs spread for balance.

"What's this she's wearing?" Maylene demands.

"And a good morning to you, too, Auntie M," I say. I take a swig from my coffee mug and glance over at Beatrice. So what? Her blouse is inside out. Does it really matter out here on the farm? Then I notice she's got her underwear on over top of her pants. All right. That, I admit, I probably shouldn't have missed. But they are almost the same color.

Beatrice is genuinely nervous now, but manages to smile sweetly up at Maylene. "You've gotten to be such a big girl," Beatrice says. "You're even bigger than George." Half the time Beatrice thinks I'm my dad when he was young, the other half of the time it seems she doesn't know who the hell I am. Which is okay. I'm not totally sure on this either.

"Come on," Maylene says, raising her voice, and sticks her hand out to Beatrice, a gold rope bracelet dangling from her wrist. "Let's get you changed," she practically shouts, even though Beatrice's hearing isn't that bad at all. Beatrice's soft, wrinkled face drops, of course. It's embarrassing, being talked at like that. I watch as Beatrice lets herself be led into the house by her daughter. The screen door bangs—shooting me straight back to when I came here to spend long weekends in the summer, painting at my little easel next to Beatrice's drafting board. Running down the trail to go swimming in the pond when it got too hot in the afternoons. Those memories are all stored right in the sound of that door thwaping shut. You can't open those days ever again. And it's killing me. This is why I think Beatrice is on to something.

I follow them in the house and wait in the living room while Maylene drags her mother up into the bedroom. What I love here is that nothing has changed since I was a kid, except that everything's shrunk down some. No matter what Maylene might have tried, there is no ugly sectional, no recliners with drink coolers attached, no wide-screen television.

I hear Maylene's voice from upstairs. "No, this way. Here, give me your arm!" I imagine her strapping Beatrice up in a straitjacket.

Beatrice kept the old, falling-apart, American primitive furniture, with coffee-stained, fifty-year-old seat cushions and missing dowels. The ratty blanket she knit herself is still thrown over the back of the couch. And there are built-in bookshelves lining the walls. There are shelves of books in every single room in this house, even the bathroom. I mean, this is a place you can really live in. There is no time here. You can dig your own rabbit hole and disappear down it. Maylene comes clomping down the stairs with Beatrice trailing behind, unhappy in a sundress. Like all these women who wear a lot of jewelry and too much perfume, you can tell Maylene thinks of herself as glamorous. And the brightly colored plaid dress she's wearing with the suspender type straps was probably called "country chic" or whatever in the catalog she ordered it from. But what with that, the hair dyed red and puffed out with spray, the heavy eye makeup and lipstick, she looks basically like a rodeo clown. She's the one who needs to be re-dressed.

"Haven't you noticed how distended her belly is?" Maylene says to me. "I asked when was the last time she went to the bathroom and she couldn't remember."

I hate it when she talks about Beatrice in front of her like she's a dog, so I don't answer. Besides, Beatrice can't remember anything. Maylene storms past me into the kitchen. I listen to her banging cupboards, rattling bottles of pills and running water while Beatrice stands in the middle of the living room, her eyes darting around like she's missing something she's pretty darn sure one of us stole. She grabs a handful of her sun dress and balls it up in her fist.

"What time is it?" she asks.

I look at the clock on the wall behind her. "It's nine-thirty," I say. I have to get a digital clock because she can't read the round ones anymore.

.   "She's probably not drinking enough water," Maylene calls from the other room, and then comes back with a glass of water and a pill and starts shoving them at Beatrice, practically yelling, Take this! Drink this! Do this! Do that! Like she'd try anything she could think of to get a peaceful little old lady all pissed off. You can tell Maylene used to be a nurse by the way she so thoroughly does not give a shit about anybody. She's always just doing the rounds. Trying to get it over with.

"She gets backed up if she doesn't drink enough water," Maylene says, turning to me. "If you want to do this, you're going to have to keep an eye on these things."

While Maylene's back is to her, Beatrice, after a furious examination of the pill in her hand, tosses it over her shoulder. It makes a tick when it hits the wall, then drops behind the couch. Beatrice sets the glass of water on a lopsided stack of magazines on an end table and then goes over to the front window. Good for her, I'm thinking.

"You think this is funny?" Maylene asks me. "Do you even know what day it is?"

I snort at Maylene and try to make my face serious again. "Gimme a break," I say, then stand there wondering what day it is.

"Well then, when were you planning to take her over to the center?"

That means it must be Tuesday. Or Thursday. Those are the days Beatrice goes to daycare. Beatrice turns from the window to face us. "Do you know what time it is?" she asks.

"Nine-thirty," I say.

"Did you drink all your water?" Maylene asks.

Beatrice decides right then to make an escape. She darts across the room quicker than you'd think a person in her eighties might be able to, but before she gets to the door, she bumps the end table and the glass of water goes to the floor. This slows her down and Maylene jumps in front of her, tells Beatrice to hold it right there, then picks up the glass and goes to get more water. I would never treat a great children's book illustrator like this, even if she was my mother.

Most people don't know it, since she let Stanley take all the credit, but Beatrice helped do a lot of the drawings for the books he wrote. The older she gets, the more she seems to be turning into one of the Pixies she used to draw. The Pixies all had long skinny arms, skinny legs with knobby knees, and round little bellies. That's how Beatrice is now. And she's shrinking, though of course she's taller than the six to twelve inches high that was as tall as the Pixies ever got. And I kind of think of her as one of those little Pixies. So maybe this was why I hadn't noticed her growing paunch, which I can see now does press out from her dress like she's smuggling a soccer ball.

Maylene comes back in with another glass of water, squares off with Beatrice again, and she means to stand there and watch Beatrice finish the whole thing. Beatrice holds the water in her hand while Maylene keeps going, "Drink! Drink!"

"What's with you and all this water?" Beatrice finally says, raising her voice too now. She's going to get hysterical if Maylene doesn't cut it out.

The Heart of It All

"You need it, Mother," Maylene says.

"I think you're trying to drown me," Beatrice says. She plunks the half-full glass down on the coffee table.

Then Maylene exhales, slaps her plaid thighs and says she wonders why she even tries. Then she says, "Let's get going." And I argue with her out the door, down the porch steps and halfway down the front walk, about which of us is going to take Beatrice to daycare, since, according to Maylene, I should have left fifteen minutes ago if I was going to do it.

Beatrice stops in the middle of the walk and says, "Wait a minute."

"What?" I ask.

"I'm kind of thirsty," Beatrice says. She says she's going to get a drink of water before she's going anywhere. Turns around and heads back to the house.

"You know, if you wanted to remind me about daycare you could've just called," I tell Maylene.

"I did," she says. "Last night and this morning. There was no answer."

Now I remember I turned off the ringer yesterday afternoon because we kept getting calls from these obnoxious telemarketers. If you don't watch, Beatrice will chat with them for half an hour, buy season tickets to theaters she's never going to go to, and change her long distance service three times a week. When I first got here, she was getting all kinds of technology and sports magazines in the mail.

Maylene goes over to her SUV and gets a cell phone out of the bag on the passenger's seat. "I'm already going to be late for my first appointment," she says, jabbing at numbers on the phone. "This is going to screw up my whole day."

"So you doing a lot of four-wheeling these days?" I ask, nodding at her SUV, which can't be a year old.

She ignores me while she slips into a whole other personality to talk to whoever picked up on the other side of the satellite. Like the SUV, and especially like the headsets everybody wore in the '80s, the cell phone is just another dislocation device. I can't stand it. I mean, why can't people just be where they are?

If you ask me, Maylene went about being a nurse the way you might go about being a call girl. She quit as soon as she'd snared a doctor and now she dabbles in that most stereotypical of piggy pastimes, real estate.

"So are you growing a beard?" she asks, folding up her nifty phone. My hand goes to my jaw and Maylene kind of laughs. "It's like there's two of you now," she says, smiling. Times like this, I like her, almost. She at least cared enough to come over here.

"Do you plan to get a job, or are you on vacation here?" she asks.

"I've got something lined up," I say. But I don't, really. I'm probably going to work for this greedy bastard I worked for several years ago. He's got an ad in the paper. "But for right now I'm taking care of Beatrice," I say. "I have to figure out how I'm going to work around that."

"Don't worry about it," Maylene says. "When we find the right facility, we're going to place her in a home."

"A home?" I say. "This is her home. You want to put her in an institution."

"John, she needs special care."

"And I'm her special grandson."

"Pretty soon she's going to need someone there for her twenty-four hours a day."

"I'm not busy," I say. "I hardly sleep anyway."

"She's going to need help using the toilet and taking a bath," Maylene says, and this kind of brings my trap shut. Maylene goes around, climbs up into her SUV and rolls down the window to yell at me. "So, you'll take her to daycare?"

"I already said I would."

Maylene turns the key and fires up her rig. "I made an appointment to tour an assisted living community up in Blue Ash. Maybe you and Beatrice should both come. It's going to be good for her. You'll see. Next Monday."

"I'm doing just fine taking care of Beatrice myself," I say, as Maylene shifts into gear.

"Oh, really?" she says. "Where is she right now?" Then she's gone in a gold-plated flash, her monstrous vehicle pounding the mud out of the puddles in the rutted dirt drive.

All's quiet on the farm again. I can't find Beatrice in the house. A thin line of water is running from the faucet into the basin of the kitchen sink, which is one of those big old things they made back when you had to use them to skin animals in, or wash cauldrons, or whatever. The back door is open and I see Beatrice standing a little ways off, her sundress hitched up and tucked into the attached belt thingy. Her legs are bright white in the sunshine, skinny though they're dappled-looking with cellulite. She has one hand held up to shade her eyes and she's looking out at the brown, overgrown field. As I get close, I think I hear her talking. She says something like, "You have to till it," but she stops when I come up and stand beside her. Nothing's been planted out here since Stanley died. We call this the farm, but what Beatrice and Stanley had was really a garden. But big enough they could supply all their relatives with vegetables and still sell some at Findlay Market. They had some cows and chickens too.

My parents kicked me out of the house when I turned eighteen and Beatrice always let me stay in her house as long as I wanted. She didn't make me pay rent. I could come and go like a human being and she never asked any questions.

"It doesn't look like he's going to grow much this year," Beatrice says, after a minute.

At first I think she's joking, but her face is serious. "I don't think so," I say.

She looks up at me and smiles, brown borders around her lower teeth. Up close, especially in the sunlight, you can see what makes her cheeks so ruddy is all the broken capillaries. The Pixies all have rosy round little cheeks like this. I smile back.

"Is that dress uncomfortable?" I ask. The purple veins on the skin make her legs looks like marbled cottage cheese.

She looks down at her dress and sighs like it's a naughty child clinging to her. "Yes," she says.

"You want to change into your pants and then we can go?" I suggest.

"I suppose," she says. I take her hand and we walk back to the house. I'm not self-conscious about doing this, like I would be with just about anybody else. Because it's the same way she used to take my hand when I was little. She knew my dad was giving me a tough time and she'd often find me sulking somewhere near where we are now, usually down by the pond. She would take my hand and lead me back to the house, give me cookies, make some iced tea for us and get me to play a few hands of gin rummy with her until I was in a better mood. Or she'd set up my kid's easel next to her drafting board and I'd work on a painting while she worked on a Pixies book illustration.

I finally get her settled in the passenger seat of her old boat of a car, get in myself, and then realize I don't have the car keys. Beatrice kept driving off, sometimes late at night, so I had to start hiding the keys on top of one of the kitchen cabinets. While I'm in the house, I remember to turn the phone ringer back on. The second I do, it rings.

"Hey what's up," Gary says. I know it's him by the stoned tone. Far as I can tell, Gary's been stoned his entire life. One of his hobbies is taking two or three hits in rapid succession, and then standing up real fast so he passes out and falls over.

"I saw you called," he says. Gary doesn't like answering the phone either. He checks his caller ID once in a blue. I called him two days ago.

"Yeah, I've got a mission for us," I say.

The Heart of It All

"Cool," he says. The good thing about Gary is he's always up for some mischief.

"Operation billboard," I say. "Look, I gotta be somewhere right now. I'll tell you about it later. Will you be home tonight?" He says he will. "Well pick up your frickin' phone for a change," I say.

Thinking I'd surprise Gary when I first got into town, I found out where he was living in Clifton, a Nasty neighborhood near UC, and then knocked on the door of his apartment. "Hey, what's up," he said. Not like he hadn't seen me for five years, just like it had been maybe five days.

That's when it really hit me how much slower time moves here. If you look around the area a little, you see some strange things. Almost all the white men walk around looking like their moms just dressed them for Sunday school. They go to church regularly. They don't talk to black people, who only live in the ghetto. People here are married by age twenty, start pumping out their dozen kids rapid-fire, and everybody is middle-aged before they're thirty. Pretty soon you realize what's going on is that you're in a time warp. It's actually still the early 1950s here.

Gary is exceptional. He copped-out altogether. After talking to him for a while when I first got to town, I found out he hadn't been doing much of anything in the time I'd been gone, unless you count making sure people get their pizzas on time. We got to talking about college because it's where we met. I threw in the towel after a year. Kept going to the parties though—they were free. I hadn't known it, but Gary kept right on going till he got his BA. This, it turned out, was a nine-year enterprise for Gary.

"Dude, it took you *nine* years?" I said, taking the bong he passed me. I really don't get high anymore. This was just a pass-the-peace-pipe-for-old-times-sake kind of thing.

"Yeah," Gary said, absently flicking a lighter. "The first five years were great. But man, those last four years sucked." He told me he'd majored in psychology. Which I guess he's decided not to practice, especially not on himself.

Back in the car, as I start down the driveway, I say to Beatrice, "It's kind of like the Spanish Inquisition when Maylene drops by, isn't it?"

"More like Chinese water torture," she says, totally deadpan. This is what Maylene doesn't even know—that Beatrice has a sense of humor.

When I laugh, I glance over and see, in the valley of Beatrice's sundress between her knees, there's a little hill of confetti growing. She must have started this while I was in on the phone with Gary. She's adding to it with whatever it is that's in her hands. I swing the car out onto the main road and look at the clock on the dash. It's not that late. If I step on it, Beatrice probably won't even miss the warm-up exercises.

Maylene's always been a fascist about schedules, which I guess she picked up as a nurse. The new SUV reminds me that she had a Mercedes when she was still nursing. She lived beyond her means even before she married the quack. Come to think of it, it was probably Pixie money she was living off. Back in the day, those books were real popular. I think Beatrice still gets royalty checks.

At a stoplight I see Beatrice is almost finished with her shredding project. I also notice the door to the glove box is hanging open. I think, Oh shit.

I point at the pile of confetti. "All right if I take a look at some of these?" I ask.

"Certainly," she says, confidently, and keeps tearing up stuff like this is her new job.

What I'm looking at in my hands is tiny bits of vehicle registration mixed up with pieces of receipts and other papers. Somebody behind me honks because the light is green.

"Hey, can you do me a favor?" I ask, as we start moving again.

"Mhmmm."

"Could you put all that back in the glove box when you're done?"

"Of course," she says.

The Heart of It All

Beatrice and I haven't missed a thing. We take the two empty chairs waiting for us in the circle. Everybody is sitting with their arms straight out in front of them, flapping their hands around as some Tchaikovsky plays at a volume a bit too high to be background music. Beverly nods at us and smiles. There's no chance of this ever happening in a million years, and it's really surprising to me—because if you had to describe Beverly's looks in one word, the best you could do is to say matronly—but I'd fuck her in a second.

"Let's stand up now," Beverly calls out to the circle. "We're going to really wake up those hands now and those arms," Beatrice and I rise with the rest. I like to participate because I think it makes Beatrice feel more like the daycare activities are normal, not just for people who have a problem. "Fingers now, fingers," Beverly says. We all hold our hands up over our heads and wiggle our fingers around. We touch our heads, shoulders and knees for a while. Or those of us who can. Some forget what they're doing and just stand there looking at the floor or scratching an armpit. This will be the extent of the warm-up. Beverly would never put this crowd through anything as dangerous as jumping jacks. Beatrice looks happy. I don't know if it's the effect of getting her blood moving, or seeing all her new friends again, but while we do the exercises her face gets an expression like she's being tickled. It probably wouldn't make any difference if I wasn't here, I think. I could just drop her off. But what the hell.

Cliff doesn't have to be here either, but he always stays and is usually close by his wife, Mildred. He told me he finally had to face up to the fact that she had Alzheimer's after he called her from work to remind her they were having company for dinner and she called him back like thirty-five times to ask what he'd just told her.

Bev gets out the kind of red rubber ball you use for kick-ball in elementary school and announces we're going to work on our reflexes. This is fine by me. Still sitting in the circle, we toss the ball to one another at random. None of these folks can catch very well, but it's going all right, so Beverly gets up, comes back and replaces the red ball with a beach ball. Instead of catching and throwing, all we have to do now is bat this one up in the air across the circle to somebody else.

Altogether, there are about twenty of us. Norman, the youngest of the people here with Alzheimer's, looks the most absurd batting the beach ball around because he's sitting there in a three-piece suit. He was some kind of bigwig at Proctor & Gamble, only forty-eight when his wife realized he had the disease. But he and Roger seem to be the best at this seated volleyball. For Roger, World War II is still on. He's nice. Treats me like a brother-at-arms. Is always questioning me about my regiment and asks worriedly if I'm going back to the front; his concern for my safety is very real and I appreciate that.

Winona, who has a suitcase standing next to her chair (she carries it everywhere), laughs every time the beach ball goes up in the air. Everybody, generally, seems to be pleased by this game and I'm thinking, Wow, they've really come full circle: the expressions on their faces are like two-year-olds'.

And here's where Bev makes a bad call, I think. She tosses the heavier red ball back into circulation while the beach ball is still going. So now you have to see which ball is coming at you and decide to catch-and-toss or swat. Which means trouble. Norm smoothes his tie while apparently making the executive decision to just smack the living shit out of anything that comes his way, because that's what he does to the red ball and the beach ball in the next twenty seconds.

"Slowly, slowly," Beverly says, raising her voice even more to be heard over the slightly alarmed murmurs, music, and the batting of balls. But it's a little late. The balls are going way too fast back and forth across the circle. The music has changed and there's a jaunty show tune on the tape deck behind Bev, which makes it seem even more like watching a film somebody sped up. One woman, a frail little thing named Deidre, isn't even with us—her head is turned so she can gaze out the window. Norm swats a line drive with the red ball in and beans her right in the side of the head. Her whole body jerks sideways and her glasses go skidding across the floor. She looks around at us, blinking.

Beverly makes a little gasp, then says, "Okay, okay! Stop! Let's stop for a minute." She gets up to turn off the music. But the red ball bounces across the floor right back to Norm like he's playing against a backboard and he winds up smacks it again. This time it flies across the room and hits the wall. The beach ball comes to Beatrice and she sends it sailing high in the air across the circle again. Then she turns to me and says, "This is kind of stupid."

I squeeze her bony shoulder as I get up to go help Deidre, who still looks like she was just rudely woken up. I notice that Beverly's assistant, Joanne, isn't here today. I pick up Deidre's glasses and hand them to her.

"Oh, thank you she says," and smiles. She seems okay. Might have even forgotten what just happened.

Beverly has managed to gather the balls and get them out of sight. If nothing else, her reflexes exercise started up some conversation. Everybody is chattering away.

"It landed right in my lap!" a woman named Grace says to Norm.

"And our earnings this quarter are up fifteen percent," Norm says, with authority. "Fifteen per*cent*."

Bev stands in the middle of the circle and I can't help noticing how her polka dot print dress bulges out at the hips. "Okay, everyone, why don't we move on to choir practice," she says over the other voices.

Beverly's preparing this group for a series of international concert engagements that will kick off at Carnegie Hall. No, not really. I mean, she's getting them ready for a few recitals she's trying to get scheduled at nursing homes and the dementia wards of hospitals in the area. Bev wants to inspire hospital staff and administrators to do more of the kinds of activities she does with Alzheimer's patients. She says it staves off the mental degeneration.

I don't know about this. From what I've seen, hospital administrators aren't the most likely folks to be inspired. About anything. Unlike Joanne, Beverly's not the type to lecture you about Jesus or anything, but she seems pretty churchy and a little naive. And you're setting yourself up if you go around expecting goodwill out of everybody.

People with Alzheimer's aren't necessarily the best harmonizers in the world. But it's amazing how a guy who doesn't recognize his own kids can remember every single word of some goofy old song. Beverly starts out with "You Are My Sunshine." Norm is the only one who doesn't sing. He keeps the beat pretty well though, with a cowbell. We let Harvey have the triangle to ding now and then because he's kind of spacey and tends to wander around. The triangle seems to help him focus. But sometimes he'll ding it between songs or even when we're not doing choir at all. The whole group will be sitting around a table, helping to make cookies or whatever and all the sudden, "Ding!" You turn around and Harvey's standing there holding the triangle aloft, a beatific expression on half of his haggard old face—the other side was deflated by a stroke.

While they're singing "Down by the Old Mill Tree," I notice Deidre's glasses are crooked; the frame must have been bent when she was hit. It makes her look all cockeyed, but she doesn't seem to notice, just sings right along, rattling a tambourine now and then.

After choir practice there's some time for people to do what passes for socializing. Beatrice starts to gravitate toward Phil, this decrepit old guy who's so far along with the disease he's almost catatonic. He barely just shuffles around. For some reason he's interesting to Beatrice. She starts patting at her hair, which is always back in a bun, whenever she sees him. Sometimes she takes Phil's arm to guide him wherever he's going. I'm guessing she uses him as a part-time stand-in for Stanley.

I don't know why Cliff asks my advice, except that he wants a second opinion. Because he's been taking care of Mildred for years and I only just started looking after Beatrice. To be polite, he always asks how it's going with Beatrice first and I say not bad, then ask him about Mildred so he can get whatever it is off his chest.

"I'll tell you, a frightening thing happened last night," he says.

"What's that?"

"Well, before dinner Mildred always gets a little antsy—someone in my support group says it's called sun-downing—around sunset they get more agitated, you know."

I don't know, but I nod.

"And last night she started saying she wanted to go home. 'We are home,' I kept telling her. But she insisted, even started to get a little hysterical, screaming over and over, 'I want to go home, I want to go home.' She was terrified. I felt awful, but what could I do?"

This is an easy one, seems to me. "Next time just say okay, take her out in the car, drive around for a little while and then come back home."

Cliff considers this, massaging his jowls. "You think that would work?"

"I don't know," I say.

Beverly goes in the kitchen to get a snack ready, and since Joanne isn't around I go in to help. Beverly is leaning into the fridge. She's wearing stockings and I hear the shushing of the sheer material of her dress as it slides over her rump. I have an instant hard-on. I don't get it— I mean, she doesn't look anything like Carla. Beverly has a generous, wide build, an oval face, pale skin and this sort of '80s feathered-back strawberry blond hair. Her shoulders are thick and her elbows are rounded with the extra padding that comes down along the backs of her arms. There's this Mother-Gooseyness about her. I wonder what the hell she'd do if, while she's still bent over into the fridge, I crouched down, lifted up her dress, stuck my head up under it and went, "Cock-a-doodle-do!"

I try to concentrate on putting the bite-sized triangles of sandwich onto plates and pouring juice into plastic cups. Beverly talks about how she's worried they're not ready for the first recital, which is in only a couple of weeks. I appreciate what Bev is doing for these people. I really do. That's how I know that what I am is a lousy, perverted son-of-a-bitch. Because I think some of what I'm attracted to, under all that squeezable flesh, is her simple, warm-hearted, goody-two-shoes personality. And what I want is to take advantage of it. I imagine her moaning, her eyes closed, lying back on this wobbling kitchen table while I ram myself into her. I must be a bad person. This is terrible. I'm like everybody else who's screwing up the whole world.

I'm getting ready to take a tray of plates out to the tables in the other room. Beverly touches my wrist. "Thanks for helping," she says. "It's so good of you to do this."

She has real pretty eyes—pale, clear blue shot through with darker streaks. I look down at my tray. "Oh, no problem," I say. I can feel myself blushing. She touched me! Jesus Christ—if she could see all the shit I'm thinking about her she'd arm herself with a butcher knife and call the cops.

At the end of the day, while I'm driving us home, Beatrice hums softly to herself, content as always after daycare. I look out at the ruined landscape. Patascala County used to be all woods and farms. They didn't have four-lane roads, these giant ice-cube-tray office buildings, chain restaurants and whatnot. All this crap everywhere must be driving Carla insane. "For Development" and "Available" signs sprout everywhere that hasn't already been what they call developed, by which they mean destroyed. "Duke Weeks Corporation," says one sign.

"Dick Weeds," I say.

Beatrice stops humming for a second, leans toward me with a smile, as if I just told her that the weather is gorgeous. The skin around her eyes crinkles. "Yes," she says, merrily.

The Heart of It All

What they've done to this rural area in just five years is shocking. For Carla it must be worse, because she's been around here all this time. When she drives on this same road we used to take out to the farm when we first started seeing each other, she must feel like I've died. Actually, I kind of feel like I've died. We used to drive out here, sometimes with a few friends, zooming through cornfields; we'd take our six packs and our pot out to the pond and go skinny dipping all afternoon and all night. We'd bring sleeping bags and sleep right there under the stars. In Stanley and Beatrice's books, while everyone else was asleep, the Pixies had the world to themselves and could run around doing whatever they wanted. So now for Carla to drive out here and see this gradual desecration of our world, it must really make her sick.

We'd always stop and visit with Beatrice before we went frolicking in the wilderness. Without fail she was glad to see us and stuffed us full of cookies and brownies and then shooed us down to the pond. Whenever she got a chance, she pulled me aside and told me to stop fooling around and marry Carla.

I look at Beatrice now, when we come to a stoplight. Carla and I are ancient history that Beatrice doesn't even know she once knew. Looking past her, I see a smug suit in a fancy car adjacent to us, with all the windows rolled up even though it's perfectly nice out. Beyond him is the enormous and depressing asphalt front lawn of one of those warehouse stores that make you listless and nauseated when you walk around in them. I hope maybe I'll catch some Alzheimer's from Beatrice.

There are these three particular billboards I've had my eye on. In one night, we should be able to get all three of them and maybe more if we want because they're pretty close to each other. They're all on interstate 75, so people can see them on when they're driving back to their subdivisions at the end of the day. I checked it out. The billboards are all on these long poles. They have ladders that start about twenty feet up the pole to keep assholes like me from climbing them.

Gary's stoned when he picks me up, so after I explain all that to him, he says, "Okay, but why're you throwing all this rope in my car?"

"So I can tie you down to the railroad tracks, man, whattaya think?"

Three o'clock in the morning is a nice time to be on the road because you hardly see anybody. Gary's quiet now because he gets offended if you say something that makes him think he's stupid. I crack a beer in the silence while he drives. The beer helps. It's one thing to imagine these operations, but actually doing them gives you the heebie-jeebies and messes with your bowels.

Gary's body has changed over the years. He doesn't look fat, just generally thicker all around. It's not a nice thing to think, but it's true: he has become thick of mind and body. Pot will do that. Pot and pizza. If you look close at Gary's forehead you can see a tiny little lump over his right eyebrow. He's damn lucky he didn't lose his eye. One time, when we were living in a house we shared with a few other guys, Gary tossed a bottle in a fire in the back yard. It exploded and in about five seconds Gary's face looked like somebody had emptied a can of dark red paint on it. He was on one of his hiatuses from school and didn't have health insurance, so we washed him up and it seemed like we'd got all the pieces of glass out, but that one is still there under the lump.

Gary is the only person I know who can drive and roll a joint at the same time. Once he's got it lit, he holds it out to me. I belch and crumple my beer can. "Like I really need to be more paranoid right now," I say. He shrugs and keeps smoking.

What's pretty unfunny is that the people in the neighborhood where the billboards are couldn't ever afford most of the crap that's advertised on them. They live in these crumbling brick shotgun houses right on the interstate and they are so broken that they let some company put a billboard right smack on the side of the sad house. Got to love that entrepreneurial spirit! I mean, the hell with carrying around a sandwich board if you can just live in one. That is capitalism and you had better fucking enjoy it or else.

You can smell the noxious melty plastic odor of the recycling plant from where we park the car near the stem of the first billboard, which grows out of a lot that's vacant except for all the garbage in it. I have to take a leak by some scrawny dead trees.

Gary's going, "I don't know about this man, I really don't know about this."

"You shouldn't've smoked that joint, you idiot," I say in a hushed voice. He's making me so fucking nervous I can barely piss. It's chilly out, and steam rises from my stream once I get it started. There are houses on the other side of the street but they're all dark. Every time a semi thunders by above us on 75, I wonder how people can live around here. It's where you'd expect a nocturnal ogre to live. And what if you have kids? Are you going to tell them that one day they could be the president of the United States if they want to bad enough? Wrong. No way. There is so much they can't do it's hard to even imagine it all. While I'm zipping up, I get a piss shiver that's so violent it's almost a convulsion.

I get the rope out of the back seat and sling on an old backpack of mine I found at Beatrice's. Once upon a time, this bag contained textbooks and now it's full of cans of spray paint. Gary is jitterbugging all around the car and by accident he kicks a broken bottle halfway across the street. I don't know what he's so nervous about since I'm the one taking the real risk. He's just the lookout. I'd call him the getaway car driver except his car is a 1970 Mercury and doesn't get much over sixty-five miles per hour. When it does, the whole thing shakes so much Gary and I are like a pair of dice in a cup.

Earlier today I tied a grappling hook onto the end of a piece of rope and tied a bunch of knots in the rope so it'd be easier to climb. I'm throwing the hook and trying to get it to catch on the bottom rung of the ladder, but I keep missing. Gary's running his hand through his mop of hair, still saying he doesn't know about this.

"Look," I finally tell him, "if we get caught, pretend you don't know who I am." I throw the hook and it clangs against the metal billboard pole and falls to the ground. "You can just say you happened to be driving by here and stopped to see what I was doing." I bend over to pick up the hook for another try.

Gary didn't used to be scared of anything. It was his idea, freshman year, to steal the sack of oranges that the kid from Florida's mom sent him, and from our dorm's hall window seven stories up, rain down about a dozen angry oranges on the cop car, then peg the cop who got out of it, then run and hide in Gary's girlfriend's room until the cop came into the building, then go out and fill the cop's glove compartment with more oranges.

I finally get the hook on the ladder and start going up.

"Be careful," Gary says.

"Shut up," I say, in a tone that lets him know I mean, Thanks. I've been trying to act like I do this all the time, but I've only done it twice before, when I was in LA. But those times I was with a group, we were all completely, blissfully ripped, and we didn't have to do a ropes course like this. Once I'm up there, I realize that wearing black pants and a black jacket doesn't make me so invisible anymore. Actually, it's pretty dumb. The billboard is white, and what with the footlights shining up on me, I'm as obvious to anyone driving by as a Hollywood hack playing Hamlet in front of a blank movie screen.

I move quick. I paint my special message in the biggest letters I can, wishing I'd chosen something shorter the whole time I'm doing it, then I get the hell back on the ground before I have a chance to shit my pants.

"Gimme one," I say to Gary, who's puffing demonically on a

cigarette as he starts the car. My hands are shaking as I light the cigarette. We go around and get on the ramp to go north on 75. Now we're just like regular people who happen to be on the road real late. What, vandalism, officer? Us? Gosh no! Oh. Well, see, it's like, um, we keep this rope and spray paint handy for odd jobs.

The billboard advertises one of those huge SUVs like Maylene drives. Under a picture of the thing, it said, "Go Further." Now it says, "Go Further—Go Greenhouse." You can tell by how the letters get a little skinnier and scrunched together that I was running out of room at the end. But it's legible. When Gary sees it at first he's just quiet. Then he starts laughing and so do I. We keep laughing until he gets off at the next exit and we go back around to drive by it again. It's so funny, Gary gets an idea. He wants to do the next one.

It's an advertisement for this grocery store called Big's. There's a picture of all these filled-up grocery bags and underneath that it says "Save Big." When Gary gets done with it, it says, "Save Big Tits." That one is so funny we have to drive by it four times, till my stomach is sore from laughing. Then Gary gets the idea a cop could see us keep driving past and figure we'd done it, and that sobers us up right quick.

We have to go a little further away from town to get to the third one I want. This one isn't near any buildings. We go down a dirt road between the highway and the railroad tracks. The billboard has a picture of a predatory-looking SUV leaving a paved road and going into a jungle. It says, "Go Ahead. Satisfy Your Instincts," under which I'm going to write, "Rape Mother Earth." But as soon as I get done the "Mother," the can I'm using starts to run out and I hear Gary. "Get down!" he's calling in a strangled voice.

"Why?" I call. I look down to where his voice is coming from, but I get blinded by the floodlights and can't see anything at all. I want to finish, but I climb down instead. There's a pair of headlights coming down the dirt road toward us.

"We're fucked," Gary says. We get in the car and start going further down the dirt road without turning on our lights.

"I can't see shit," Gary says. But that's not exactly true. There's enough light from the streetlights on 75 above us to basically see where the two tire grooves of the dirt road are. I look back and the headlights are getting closer. They seem to be shaped like cop headlights but I'm not sure about that.

"Where does this go?" Gary asks.

"I don't know," I say.

"Aw, fuck, dude—you said you did recon, man. We are totally fucked."

"It's probably just some people coming back here to screw in their car," I say.

"Yeah, cops. They're going to screw us."

I crane my neck around again and see the headlights getting steadily closer. "We'll pretend we're lost," I say. This has been my strategy for life. It's worked so well I really am completely lost now.

Then there's a mini-miracle. In Beatrice and Stanley's books, the Pixies always just barely manage to escape being seen by people. At the break of dawn, a farmer might think he hears giggling and a lot of little scurrying footsteps in his barn. But just as he swings the door open, the Pixies all dive behind bales of hay or into barrels, and its normal and quiet when the farmer walks in. Then he hears mooing up over his head and when he looks up, there's one of his cows that somehow got stranded up in the loft. He takes off his cap, scratches his head and says, Sweet Jesus, and, I'll be damned, and, Nelly, how on God's green earth did you manage to get up there, and so forth. He doesn't know the Pixies were experimenting with pulleys and a harness they made because they'd found a book that had diagrams showing how to do this stuff. But they've hidden all the evidence. As the farmer climbs the ladder to the loft, all the Pixies slip out the door and go running through the field into the woods where they climb up tree trunks and disappear into knotholes. But in the Pixies' world, when you climb into a knothole in a tree there's a living room and kitchen and bedrooms and a fireman's pole you can slide down to get from one floor to the other. The Pixies just sleep all day in their tree houses.

So what happens is we come to a place where you can keep going straight along the railroad tracks or turn left, onto a different dirt road, and go under 75, which is what we do. And we're trapped. This isn't a road; it doesn't go anywhere. There's a hill that goes up on the other side of the highway into the trees. We do the only thing we can, which is turn off the car and hope they go by us. The engine ticks. It's starting to get light out.

"Let's leave the car here and run for it," I say. But Gary isn't having any of that. So we wait. There are more cars on the interstate than there were earlier. We can hear them whoosh by above us. I have on a glow-in-the-dark digital watch that shows it's 5:30. People on their way to work already? They must be helplessly insane. In the rearview mirror, I can see the dirt road behind us getting lit gradually by the car that was behind us. I feel my heart thumping, the blood flooding into my thighs, telling me to get the fuck out of the car and run. There's a flash, and the car goes by so fast I can't even tell if it's a cop car or not. After a few minutes, Gary starts the car and we slowly go back out the way we came.

2

When I worked for Ryan Rinckel before, I made the mistake of mentioning I'd taken Spanish in high school. This is what he's all excited about when I talk to him on the phone. Apparently he's got a lot of Mexican slave labor now. But his enthusiasm is so real, I start feeling proud of myself and make the same mistake all over again by telling him I got a chance to brush up on my Spanish when I was processing salmon on a trawler in Alaska, where I worked mostly with Mexicans.

"Great John, this is great," he says. He has a real nasally voice. "You can be my interpretator. When can you come in for an interview?"

This seems a tad formal for a job planting trees and pruning shrubs, which I did for him several years ago. I say, "Interview, Ryan? Don't you remember what I look like?"

"Yeah, well you can fill out the paper work and we can have a talk about the role you'll be playing on the team."

Team. Holy shit. The last time I heard that was during the five-day training program I had to endure so I could sell people caffeine from a corporate coffeehouse. Ryan sure has changed, I think, as I drive into the Nasty for this "interview." He sounded so practically busting with aggressive good cheer, it was kind of alarming. He used to always be either drunk or hung-over, and was always yelling his head off at anybody he thought might be mistreating a shovel he'd paid good money for.

Because the rent is so cheap, Ryan keeps his shop in the Walnut Hills neighborhood, which I see, driving through, has slipped even further downhill in the years I was gone. A lot of abandoned buildings with charred black holes for windows. What people here do is sit on steps and watch cars go by. It's sad. They really don't have any idea what to do. It's like this all along Vine Street down the hill to downtown. This is the Over -the-Rhine neighborhood (a.k.a. Ghettover-the-Rhine). Get over it. If you can. You might get jumped, though. These young guys, they're just hanging there in front of condemned buildings like rotting fruit. This is not how I like to imagine it is along the actual Rhine River.

Ryan's office is a little trailer attached to the warehouse across the street from the pit, a big lot where we dump debris and where he keeps piles of manure, mulch, gravel, palates of stone, the chipper and the Bobcat. I remember working this one job where a little kid kept coming up and asking us when we were going to use the baby bulldozer, and that was what we called the Bobcat the rest of that year. The fence around the pit is twice as high as the one Ryan used to have, and now it's got a spool of razor wire along the top. But there's a brand spanking new white pickup in front of the warehouse with a new logo—a picture of a big leaf with the words "Ryan Rinckel, Inc. Landscaping" on it. Okay, I get it: he turned over a new leaf. This could even mean no more planting dead maples in people's yards and telling them it just needs water and some time.

The realization of how badly I do not want to do this hits me with the first whiff of pesticides that greets me when I open the door. The chemicals are all in a closet in this room and it's the dormant oil in particular that makes you think you better hold your breath the whole time you're in here to keep from getting cancer.

"Hey buddy," Ryan says. He comes around the desk to shake my hand. There's something different about him. He's lost weight but that's not it. Probably quitting drinking made his face look different. Looking at him, I try to imagine putting my own name inside a leaf and putting it on the left breast of a bright white polo shirt and then wearing it, which is what he's done. This must be the kind of thing that Ryan thinks commands respect, even if it doesn't receive it.

After some shit about how long it's been, I sit down across the desk from him. The desk is scarred by cigarette burns and slashes—some I remember making with my pruners when I was pissed off about something that must have mattered to me about six years ago.

"Now, the way I'm lookin' at this for you," Ryan says, his elbows on the desk, "is you're in kind of a pinch-hitter position here."

Through the new bars on the window behind Ryan, I see a girl who can no way be more than fifteen, pushing a stroller. Maybe cutting school to babysit for an older sister? Yeah right!

"What I'm gonna do is put you on whichever crew needs your particular skills at the time," Ryan says. "When the amigos get here, sometimes you'll be running your own crew." I guess he decided "the amigos" is a more politically correct abbreviation for labor he hardly has to pay for than "the illegal aliens."

When he's concentrating real hard, Ryan's eyebrows move up and down and the muscles in his forehead make it look like his brain is squirming around there just under the skin. I'd forgotten about this, and when I'm looking at it, I notice the other thing. What's making him look so different now. The hairpiece. It's got flecks of fake gray in it to match the hair on the sides, but it doesn't quite do the job. The problem is I can't quit looking at it, examining the border where the real stuff ends and the synthetic stuff starts. And wondering how it's attached.

I try to stare into his eyes the way he's staring into mine. When he pauses, I say, "Well, you could pay me extra for my expertise."

All the good humor evaporates and his face goes blank for a second. I feel so bad for him—once a nice kid who liked to mow people's lawns for money, sitting here now with his name on his shirt in this toxic, scuffed-up little room in the middle of a ghetto. Then he flashes a smile so white I wonder if he got fake teeth too. He goes, "Ha, ha, ha. We'll see about that."

The way he's looking into my eyes, I'm pretty sure now it's either to see if I'm noticing the hairpiece, or it's a stare he uses to try to keep people from looking at it. Just to see his face drop again, I think of nodding at the hairpiece, and saying, "Hey Ryan, you mind taking the beanie off while we have our talk? It's distracting the hell outta me."

But I don't. And he starts carrying on about how great it is that I'm back, it means so much to him to have good quality workers and he really wants me to get something out of the job. "I want you to feel like it's your company too," he says, which is a heap of horseshit so huge that I gag trying to swallow a laugh. "What?" he says. He seems to be pretending I'm someone who doesn't know him. He wouldn't share a shirt with his own Siamese twin.

I tell him on account of Beatrice I can't start for a week or two yet.

"Oh, that's fine" he says. "Actually at this point I'm only sending one crew out since the weather has been somewhat remiss." I guess he means the rain we've been having. "So that's okay," he says. "We can go lazzie fare on that. It's still early in the season."

I must have looked at him funny because he says, "Don't you know that word? It's from hist'ry—it's French for procrastinating."

Whatever. I tell him that when I do start, I'm not going to want to work every day because on certain days they don't have daycare. And on those days I have to see what kind of mood Beatrice is in and decide whether it's okay to leave her or not. Then watching Ryan's face is like seeing somebody slowly let the air out of a smiley-face balloon wearing a little gray-flecked brown cap. "So I was hoping maybe we could go lazzie fare on that too," I finish up, on a hopeful note.

"That's going to screw me up with the schedules, John, you know that," he says. "I can't have flextime here. If I need four guys on a job, I don't wanna have to spend an extra day going out to finish it up because we only had three guys on it." His face gets red as it re-inflates. He's doing a good job of holding off on the swearing, though. That must be part of whatever better-business program he's following.

I guess I could say, "Well since this company is mine too, I reckon I should be able to choose which days I want to work." But the thing is, I haven't heard back from any other place I applied. Who knows—maybe they all did background checks. And that makes me nervous, so I mumble something about trying to let him know ahead of time and he shakes his head like I let him down already, and says we'll see how it goes.

I fill out the W-2 and all the other shit real quick, skip the part about, Have you ever been convicted of a blah, blah, blah, and get out of there. On my way out, on top of the file cabinet by the door, I see accessories to Ryan's problem. Two box sets of cassette tapes: "The Art of Success," and "Building a More Professional Vocabulary for a More Professional You."

When I get home, Beatrice is in her old studio in the back of the house. She's sitting at the drafting board she hasn't used for years and years, gazing out at the field through the waves and air bubbles of the ancient glass in the windows. From here, you have a view of the barn at the edge of the field, which has lost so much paint you can't tell what color it used to be. As a kid, I imagined it as a kind of night workshop the Pixies used. I would stay up as late as I could, watching out the window, waiting for them to come out of the woods. The barn slumps to the side now like a gray shipwreck at low tide.

There's a pen in Beatrice's hand and I see she's been doodling. Pieces of things that could be the ruins of the Pixies in her mind. There's something that looks like the hats the Pixies wore: just three leaves tied together at the stems with spider webbing. They were always losing their hats on their adventures, but they kept big spools of spider webbing in their tree houses, and there were always plenty of leaves around.

When she first met me, Carla couldn't believe I was related to the people who wrote the Pixies books. We were both working at this kind of fancy bookstore. It was my first job where I had to deal with the public and I was always apologizing to customers, lots of times for things that weren't my fault. I never heard Carla apologize for anything in my life. Pretty women made me feel ashamed and embarrassed, and Carla Decker made me so embarrassed that for the first week I worked there I'd always try and get this guy Doug to switch with me if I was scheduled to work with her for that hour. Every hour you moved to a different station— front register, to phone room, to children's section, to music section, and so on.

We were both scheduled to work in the phone room one afternoon on a day Doug didn't feel like switching with me again. When I went back there, she was leaning back in her chair with one leg up on the desk next to her computer. Leafing through an archeology magazine and eating a candy bar.

"Oh, hey," she said, glancing up at me. "So where's Doug?"

The phone rang; Carla took a bite of her candy bar and then picked it up. She said the name of the bookstore while she chewed, but didn't say her own name like they trained us to. She'd been working there a while. "Let me check on that," she said. She put down her candy bar, held the phone out to the computer keyboard and randomly tapped keys with her left hand. "Okay, I'm showing we have nine hundred thirty seven copies of that in stock," she said into the phone. I noticed small patches of the corduroy were worn off her pants at the thigh. She had what I think they call a swimmer's build—slim, but solid, with undefined muscles. "Sure I can," she told the customer. "Would you like me to reserve a copy? Please hold." She put them on hold, put the receiver in the cradle, and picked her magazine back up off her lap. She never picked their line up again.

I'd sat down and was looking at her, kind of dumbfounded. She noticed and shrugged. "Idiots," she said. "They're all worried about getting that cookbook the author is coming here to sign. It's not like we're going to run out." She'd tied a loose ponytail in her hair, which came down to the middle of her back. It was dark brown and shiny. It would get lighter streaks in it in the summer, but I didn't know that yet. I didn't know anything about her for sure, but the Nasty is a small place and I knew people who knew her. I guessed the stories I'd heard probably weren't true, because I knew they'd been started by East side girls who were probably jealous because Carla was so pretty and she was from the West side.

The phone rang again and I hesitated. "You don't like this, do you?" Carla said.

"It's just I screw up all the time," I admitted. "I still haven't got the hang of finding things on the computer." I was so timid in those days, I was a different person.

"Watch," she said, and picked up the phone. She repeated the title the person was looking for as she, again, randomly tapped at the keyboard of her computer. If a book turned out not to be in stock, we were supposed to look to see if it was at our warehouse, and if it wasn't there, then see if it was at the distributor. If you couldn't order it from either of those places you were supposed to order it from the publisher.

Carla bypassed the whole system. After a slightly longer period of tapping than she'd given the last caller, she said, "That book is out of print." She paused and examined her short, bitten fingernails while the person on the other end talked. "There's nothing I can do about it," she said. "It's beyond our control. Thanks for calling. Bye, bye." She hung up.

"Usually, you don't even have to go through all that," she explained to me. "It depends how serious they sound. Most of the time, you just tell them we don't carry that title."

The phone rang again and she picked it up, then noticed a copy of the schedule lying between our computers, and hung the phone right back up without saying anything. "Look at that," she said, picking up the schedule. "We're both in Children's next." Then she looked at me, fake horrified. "And Doug's shift is over! What in the world are you going to do?"

"Sweat a lot," I said, since I was too anxious to think of anything besides the truth.

"John," she said, looking back at the schedule, like she was thinking out loud. "So how's it feel to be named after the thing everybody shits on?"

In the children's section, Carla mostly browsed and let me take care of the few customers who came in. At one point, when I was straightening up the aisles because some parents had let their kids throw books all over the place, I found Carla sitting cross-legged on the floor, a picture book open on her lap, head bowed, her elbows on her knees and palms on her cheeks.

I rang up some books for a woman while her two little girls peered up at me over the edge of the counter. Per policy, I asked her did she find everything okay today? Did she have a reader's card? Did she know that with the reader's card she could get a thirty percent discount on a book once she'd spent about twenty million dollars in this place? Then I was hit right in the nose with a stuffed Babar the elephant. The little girls laughed and clapped their hands enthusiastically. The woman looked around, but Carla had ducked down behind some bookshelves already.

After they'd gone, Carla re-materialized. "You know children's books really suck these days," she said. "Have you had a chance to take a look at some of the crap we're selling?"

"Actually, I've been concentrating on helping customers," I said.

"Well, come here," she said. I followed her over to the picture books. Carla walked in a way that let you know she knew you knew she was actually a goddess. She had the tomboy grace of a professional tennis player. She showed me some books, which were selling like crazy, about this family of bunny rabbits that's always going to church and taking in poorer bunny rabbits to share Thanksgiving dinner with and stuff like that. The pictures were all cotton candy pinks, yellows and blues.

Carla leaned against the low shelf running along the wall and I noticed the indentation in her hip pressing against it. "Why do they think kids are stupid?" she said. "There's no imagination in this. Let me show you a real children's book."

She bent over and started scanning the shelf. She pulled out one of Stanley and Beatrice's books and put it in my hands. It was a recent edition of one of their first ones. A lot of stores don't even carry but one or two of them anymore. We carried them all because they were by local authors. I was surprised Carla had heard of the Pixies, since it was people our parents' age who had been brought up on them. On the cover of this one, the words "Further Adventures of the Pixies" was spelled out in Pixies all strung together and bent funny ways to form the letters. All around this was a border made of different scenes of the Pixies getting into trouble—one Pixie upside-down with his head stuck in a bucket; three Pixies on a tree limb pouring a can of paint on three other Pixies on the ground; a bunch of Pixies driving a car off a cliff, with one Pixie swinging on the handle of the open door through which you can see different ones working the gas and brake pedals and the others standing on each other's shoulders to see out the windshield and steer.

"My grandfather wrote these," I said.

Carla snorted and jerked the book out of my hands. "And I'm a Ubangi," she said. She cleared off a whole display of the bunny books, piled them on the floor and put the Pixies book on the display instead.

"No, really," I said. "My grandmother helped some with the illustrations, but it was mostly my grandfather."

"You are so full of shit," she said. "That's probably why they named you John."

"All right," I said, and started back to the register.

"Your mother's or father's parents?" she asked, following me.

"My father's."

Carla held out her hand. "Lemme see your driver's license." I got it out and she looked at it and said, "Holy shit. Your name's John Ritter."

"Yeah," I said, standing up a little straighter.

"You know what Ritter means in German?" I didn't. "It means knight," she said, which I liked, till she added, "That makes you, like, 'Knight of the Toilet.'"

3

At Carington Valley we all stand crowded around a little speaker next to the door while Maylene pushes the button to buzz the caring staff. Beatrice's eyes dart around, full of suspicion, while Sheila stands behind her looking positive and motivated and all that stuff I can't stand in anybody except her, because whenever I'm around she slips into the big-sister act she's been doing for me ever since I can remember. Somehow she managed to only inherit the good aspects of Maylene's personality. Sheila's a few years older than I am. There was this kid in grade school who always picked on me out on the playground, doing generic stuff like shoving me and calling me a pussy to get me to fight him, because he knew he could kick my ass. One day Sheila saw this happening and without a word she stepped between us, hauled off, and broke the kid's nose. He never bothered me ever again.

"We have an appointment with Melissa Perkins?" Maylene tells the perforated plastic.

"Please?" says the speaker's crackling female voice. This is peculiar to the region. Instead of "Sorry?" when they don't hear you the first time, people here say "Please?" I've heard it has to do with the translation from German, but there's no getting around the fact that it makes them sound idiotic.

"Melissa Perkins?" Maylene says. "We have an appointment to tour the facility?"

"Just a minute," the voice says, and then there are sounds of a scuffle, a grunt, and then what could be the thump of a dead body falling on a desk. The door buzzes and I hold it open for everybody. Once they're all in the foyer already, a different voice crackling from the speaker tells us to come in.

"This is like visiting a prison," I say to Sheila, as we go through the next door into what looks like the unnecessarily spacious lobby of a franchise hotel, where Melissa Perkins is smiling her way across the carpet to meet us. She's dressed the part of the PR person, but Maylene has sure outdone her. Maylene's wearing white pants and a navy blue blazer with a kind of royal gold coat-of-arms or something on the pocket so she looks like the person you'd expect to greet you when you step on a cruise ship. And it almost seems like she's the one doing the welcoming. While she and Melissa chirp to each other, I notice that there's glossy wood furniture grouped around a fireplace that has fake logs in it. It looks two-dimensional, like there should be a caption under it that says, "Cozy, home-style surroundings!" Ostensibly soothing but actually irritating music sifts down from speakers stuck in the ceiling tiles. It's the type of air-conditioned space waste that ordinarily you would just walk through real quick when you're shopping, or getting a room, or making an appointment, or whatever.

The difference is that here an old woman is sitting in one of the chairs by the phony fireplace, looking at us while she strokes a browning, stuffed Snoopy. Another old woman in a wheelchair nearby has an advanced case of some muscular disorder that makes her head roll over to the side and her arms and torso jerk around like they're being moved by somebody with a remote control. At one point she makes an especially violent movement forward and I'm sure she's going to pitch right out of her chair onto the floor. A man whose eyes peer out from dark caves in his face is sitting next to her, but doesn't seem to notice her. At the end of his armrest, his thumb keeps going in and out of his cupped hand like a nervous, naked little animal peeking out of its burrow. He keeps bobbing his head like to say, "What's up," to somebody coming down the hall. It's so convincing, I look over a couple of times but there's nobody coming.

Once Maylene finishes trying to impress Melissa, which strikes me as backwards, she introduces her to the rest of us. Melissa has a way of talking that makes it look like the words are actual objects coming out of her mouth and that disgorging them is a strenuous kind of exercise for her lips. Her smile turns all saccharine as she bends forward and clasps one of Beatrice's hands between two of hers.

"And how are you?" she asks.

"Well, I'm still alive," says Beatrice.

"Oh, ha, ha," Melissa says, but Beatrice isn't smiling, so Melissa quickly makes a painted red O out of her lips, scratches at her cheek with a ceramic fingernail, and looks distracted like she just remembered there was something she meant to pick up at the cleaners. Then she tells us to let her start showing us around.

"I thought she was the funeral director," Beatrice says, as we follow the others. She's clutching my elbow and I'm pretty glad about that. You never see her touch Maylene. The skin on Beatrice's hands looks like stretched-out latex gloves that have little folds all over them. It seems like almost nothing to have between all the hard, sharp things in the world and her delicate tendons, blue veins and swollen knuckles. Her hands are so soft but gnarled and brittle underneath, it seems like it would be difficult to do anything with them. It's hard to imagine how they helped bring all those Pixies to life.

There's not much to see out in the valley of Carington Valley. Paved walking paths and benches to stop and rest on. Before this, it was farmland, and before that, glaciers covered it, and before that, mastodons and woolly mammoths were walking around here. An old man sits on a bench with his eyes closed to the sun, like an old lizard trying to heat up its blood. His hands rest on top of his four-pronged cane. Right where he is, a giant ground sloth might once have sat, munching some prehistoric vegetation. Huge beasts that are difficult to even imagine lasted here way longer than our frail, hairless species is going to, at this rate. It's my belief that this is because those creatures were only slaves to instinct, just stupidly trying to survive; they didn't have consciousness to help them find ways to make themselves extinct.

After a minute, I can hardly stand that old codger on his bench. He makes me want to cry. I mean, it's just too much—this business of blatantly putting old people out to pasture. It's obscene. And what really places it in the horror movie genre is the chemically treated Melissa Perkins with her sprayed hair and painted face, standing here acting like a game show host presenting this corporate mausoleum as the grand prize. Where Melissa has stopped to tell us about the terrific fresh air, there's a silly lamppost made to look like an old-fashioned oil lamp except that it's plastic. I imagine taking one of the ornamental stones from the flowerbed it stands in, turning and hurling it through the plate glass window of the dining hall behind us. I imagine the old man rising from his bench, clapping and calling out, Bravo!

The grounds depress me so much, when we go back inside I hardly notice the white-trashy mammoths that work in the place and I almost get run down by one with a heap of laundry in her arms. The mammoths went to feed in these bogs and ate until they weighed so much they couldn't get themselves out of the mud, and they'd die right there. These modern versions are not much different. The whole Midwest is like this.

Melissa shows us one of the cells—a bed, a sink, a handicapped bathroom and a view of the parking lot. Prison with carpeting. While she's describing the facility, Melissa's voice rises and falls in a way that almost makes it sound like she's singing. I start to see life at Carington Valley as this nightmarish musical with the cast all dancing around with canes and walkers, singing until they collapse. Their bodies are discreetly dragged off stage by the fat staff.

"So how much will all this set us back?" I ask, as we're tagging along behind Melissa on the way to the activity room. Maylene shoots me a look like I just farted real loud, while Melissa's lips writhe all over her face. She doesn't answer my question. Instead talks about different levels of assistance and an á la carte system of service options.

There are a few defunct people sitting around in the activity room, where Melissa fills us in on bingo night and other occasions Beatrice would be able to dread if she lived here. There's a bookcase that looks like it gets cleaned instead of used, and on the polished tables there are neat displays of magazines about homemaking and crafts. I don't think Beatrice will be using the ping pong table.

I wonder what Sheila is making of all this. Her power-of-positive-thinking mask is still in place, but I like to think I see telltale cracks in it. Sheila played soccer in college and went ahead and got a degree and everything. Now she's a divorced paralegal going to law school.

Melissa and Maylene head back down the hall like storm-trooper sisters. Melissa shows us a bathroom with a special shower/tub thing for people who need help bathing. The thought of Beatrice being manhandled by one of those mastodons makes me want to smash something. In the dining room a couple of them are talking real loud about a TV show while they set the tables for lunch. Music flurries down from the ceiling in here too. A few old people are sitting at various tables, none of them saying anything. Two of them have their mouths open like this is what they do, just wait for the next meal to be put in.

The same people are still in the hearth area where Melissa's mouth goes through the contortions necessary to thank us for coming. The woman with the Snoopy doll has nodded off with her double chin on her chest, her hand around the dog's throat. Things aren't so bad, I guess; she could be sitting alone on a park bench somewhere. But in a way, this almost seems worse to me. I hope at least somebody comes to visit her.

At the last possible second, it occurs to me to ask Melissa, "Is the staff here trained to deal with people with Alzheimer's?"

She smiles like she'd been hoping I'd ask that one and proceeds to assure me—her jaw working up and down, her mouth going wider than a screaming rock star's, then getting tiny like she's sucking a small straw as she speaks—that the staff is carefully trained and that many of her residents are memory impaired. Again, I don't really get an answer, but all this overblown lip service instead.

I help Beatrice up into Maylene's SUV and get her strapped in. Of course Beatrice and I are riding in the back, like bad kids. This tank still smells like new leather inside. As Maylene pulls it out of the Carington Valley parking lot, I'm amazed as I was when she picked us up this morning. I mean, there are all these drink holders and whatnot.

"This is like driving your living room around," I say.

"You can even watch TV," Sheila says happily, turning in her seat and pointing to a screen that folds out of the ceiling. My guess is that this state of constant jubilation must only be possible if you've been hit thousands of times in the head by a speeding soccer ball.

"No thanks," I say.

"So what did you think?" Maylene demands.

"Mostly, I thought about extinction," I say. But she wants to know if I think Beatrice would be happy living there and I say she should ask Beatrice.

"I don't see why I couldn't live right here in this cabbage," Beatrice says. What's surprising is how you know what Beatrice means in spite of what she says. Like with everybody, the two don't always match.

Before I realized I was going to have to come back here and take care of Beatrice, if you asked if I was the kind of person who would be caught dead getting out of an SUV at a chain restaurant like Bob Evans, with a bunch of plastic lunch-hour people in a suburb of the Nasty, I'd have said, "Yeah right, and also I'm the highest-flying pig of porkopolis!" But here I am.

And the crazy thing is, here's Carla too, ahead of us at the hostess stand with her boyfriend. Needless to say, my appetite is gone. In fact, I'm about to throw up all over the tile floor that smells like fresh ammonia. But no, Carla would never be out here in Blue Ash. What, on her lunch break from some accounting firm? Snap out of it! Of course it's not her, as I can see now, with her profile to us as she follows the hostess to a table.

"Are you okay?" Sheila asks.

"Yeah. I just thought for a second I saw Carla."

"Don't tell me you're still thinking about her," she says. "You know she—" but the hostess interrupts to guide us through the din of dining swine to a booth, and whatever intel Sheila has about Carla remains a mystery. And I'm not going to ask, because I'm not thinking about Carla at all. Actually, I've sworn off that. About a year ago, I was talking long distance to Sheila and I accidentally mentioned Carla. But I'd really just called to see how Sheila was doing. "Forget about Carla," she said. "You two were never right for each other anyway."

"I know that," I said, and she got quiet. "What? Don't you think I know that? It's been over for years. It's ancient history. I'm glad it's over. I'm real happy now. I'm just totally fucking delighted, all right?"

I sit down in the booth next to Beatrice and across from Maylene, who opens her laminated menu and tells it, "Carington Valley seems like a fine place for Mother."

"How much does it cost?" I ask. "I noticed Ms. Perky was kind of reticent about that little detail."

"You know," Maylene says, replacing her menu on the table with a cruel precision, "a lot of these places have waiting lists. And it was certainly better than others I've seen."

"Wow, it's a magical question," I say. "Just ask anyone, and they're bound to start spewing non sequiturs."

"It's about three-thousand a month," Sheila says, then looks at

The Heart of It All

Maylene like, "Whoops."

"How much?" I ask. "I didn't see an Olympic-size pool with palm trees around it and a swim-up bar. I didn't see cocktail waitresses in string bikinis."

A guy in what could be a golfing outfit, or just Midwestern driving-to-the-mall garb, gives me a nasty look from the booth across from us. But I'm not the one with my kid throwing stuff all over the floor from a high chair while my four other kids use the booth as a jungle gym.

I'm interrupted anyway by our waitress, who has the same hairstyle Maylene has. The idea is to get it cut short, blow it back and spray stiffening chemicals on it until you look like you just spent the last hour standing in a wind tunnel. Every so often, Maylene taps at hers like she's making sure her helmet is on. That emblem on her jacket reminds me of Brad. He used to wear white collar shirts with things like that stitched on the pocket. I'll never know what the hell Carla saw in him.

The waitress takes our order and leaves us in a sour silence. I look through one of the brochures Maylene brought, and find pictures of old timers laughing their way through their last years locked up in Carington Valley. I ask Beatrice what she thought of the place.

"Just a bunch of old people, really," she says. But she's watching an older couple being shown to their table as she says this, so I don't know if she means here or there. Then I notice the muzak being piped into this place is the same as what was back there in Death Valley. And the carpeted, varnished look of this place is the same too. And the heavy hostess here could pass for one of the attendants there. Is every single place in the world exactly the same these days?

I flip the brochure over. On the back, I discover that Carington Valley is one of the many Wellington Homes across the country. In our area we have two other excellent locations to choose from: Sunny Valley and Pleasant Meadows. There's a map of the U.S. with a rash of red dots, meaning Wellington Homes, all over it.

"Holy smokes, you didn't tell me it was part of a freaking franchise," I say. "Look, it's infecting the whole country like chicken pox." I hold up the brochure.

"They've been in business for twenty-five years," Maylene says. "I think they know what they're doing."

"McDonald's been making hamburgers for a long time too," I say. "But I wouldn't want to have to eat there every single day for the rest of my life."

I realize how loud I've been talking when Beatrice starts banging something on the side of the table. She's got her shoe in her hand. Now she holds it up over her head and squints up into it. Our food comes, and Maylene looks like she's going to die of mortification. Sheila talks Beatrice into turning over the shoe while the waitress passes out our plates. By the time the waitress has gone, Sheila has gotten Beatrice's shoe back on, but now something else is the matter.

Beatrice stares at her country-fried steak like somebody just dropped some road kill in front of her. She lifts up the corner of the steak and peeks under it the way you might lift a rotten log you expect to find a lot of scurrying critters underneath. Her hand drops back into her lap. "This isn't what I ordered," she announces.

"Yes you did," Maylene says, "I heard you order that."

Wrong, I think.

"What did you order?" Sheila asks.

All wrong. Things like this can get her so tense. Beatrice's face twists up as she tries to remember what she ordered. Her mouth is puckering up now, sending dozens of little lines radiating from around it. I want to put an arm around her to comfort her, but at this point it would be a sure way to get her shouting. I'm wishing she didn't have to eat any of this factory farmed crap. She and Stan produced almost all their own food— grew vegetables, raised chickens for eggs and meat, got milk and made cheese from their own goats and cows. And Beatrice knew how to cook.

She was always experimenting with new recipes and spices. Eating dinner over at their house was like going to France.

Maylene glances quickly around and then leans forward. "Just *eat it,* Mother," she hisses.

Beatrice starts to quiver and quake. Her voice turns into a growl. "Why don't *you* eat it?" she says.

"Oh, look," I say, and make like I just noticed my plate. "They gave me yours by mistake. I remember, you ordered the hamburger, right? I ordered the steak."

Beatrice watches carefully as I switch our plates. Then she looks at me like I just performed a magic trick. "You are so," she says, then reaches out and pinches the end of my nose. She looks satisfied as she picks up the burger and sinks her dentures into it.

I give Maylene a look that I intend to mean, "See how easy that was?" But I don't think she reads it that way. She stabs angrily at her Caesar salad and we're all quiet for a little bit, while dopey music and the noise of other diners washes over us.

They call this the heartland, but they ought to change that to heartburn land or coronary thrombosis land. This woman glides by our table draped in a denim dress you could easily make five pairs of jeans out of. The dress comes so far down that her feet are hidden, and so seeing her go by is more like watching a parade float rolling through the place.

"So, you got a job," Maylene says. "When are you going to get your own apartment?"

"What would be the point of that?" I say.

Then all the sudden Maylene doesn't know where to look. Her lipstick makes a big sad-clown frown and she sets her fork on her plate. She gets a tissue from her purse and dabs at her eyes.

"I'm sorry," she says. "It's just that I feel responsible for you, for showing you how to find your way, ever since your father and mother passed." She reaches across the table and grabs my shoulder with fingers covered in sparkling metals and stones. "What can I do to help you, John? What?"

Her eyes are about to spill again. This all seems forced, but it doesn't matter. Now I feel like total crap. I mean, here she is trying to do the best she can by her mother—and by her dead brother too, by trying to give me some kind of guidance—and all I do is mess everything up. And worse, I probably remind her of her brother every time she looks at me. She lets go of my shoulder and I keep my eyes down and poke at the fried steak. What an awful idea: fried steak. Sheila asks if I've been getting out at all or just watching Beatrice. She says she wants to introduce me to some friends. She starts talking about a party she went to recently, and the way she talks about it I get the sense she's part of some singles scene.

"I don't feel very well," Beatrice says. She's eaten not only the hamburger, but all the fries that came with it. I wouldn't have guessed she could, she's so tiny.

"Have some of my soda. It'll settle your stomach," Sheila says. She empties the rest of her can into a plastic cup and pushes it across to Beatrice.

"No, don't," I say. But it's too late; Beatrice is ignoring me, already tipping it in. "The aluminum is the whole problem."

I read up on this. I know what I'm talking about. Whenever they do autopsies on people with Alzheimer's, they find nerve fiber tangles and aluminum deposits that other dead people don't have. I've been making sure to always keep a clean filter on the water tap. I threw out all Beatrice's aluminum pans and foil. I threw out all her antacids. When she asks for one, I give her a chewable vitamin C, which will help stop the aluminum from being absorbed into her system. I did an overhaul of her food, and got her eating stuff with lots of calcium and magnesium, which will also block aluminum.

On the way across the parking lot, back out to Maylene's suburban battle cruiser, I notice Beatrice's pockets are bulging. "What've you got there?" I ask, as I help her in. I slip a couple fingers into her pocket and pull out a plastic container of cream and four sugar packets.

"Those are mine," she says, grabs them and stuffs them back in her pocket.

I don't know how she managed to swipe them all without any of us seeing, but she must have a dozen creamers and forty packets of sugar on her. When Maylene drops us off, Sheila says she'll call me soon so we can go "out." Maylene reminds me she's picking up Beatrice on Wednesday, but I don't remember her telling me about this before. Something tells me I should ask where she's taking Beatrice, but I'm still feeling so ashamed for making her cry that I just want her to go away.

I don't know what's the matter with me, how I wound up a half-step from a homeless person. And with the exception of Gary, I don't know anyone else who's stuck in this state of suspended maturation. When I was little, I'd hear my dad talking to my mom about people he worked with and always calling someone or other a lousy bum. When my parents' friends were over for cocktails they'd ask me what I wanted to be when I grew up and I always told them happily, "A lousy bum." It doesn't seem nearly so funny now.

All I know is, one minute all my friends and I are driving fast, drinking, smoking, and singing along to AC-DC songs at the top of our lungs and the next minute everybody's got nonsensical jobs, and no time for nonsense. Seems the one game most people never get tired of playing is grown-up.

Carla and I were going to be different. She told me how the Australian aborigines had no concept of time in their culture. We were lying under the stars on a summer night down by the pond. I asked how could you not have time. Carla rolled from her side onto her back. We'd just gotten out of the water and I could feel the goose bumps on her skin when I put my hand on her tummy.

"They see events as existing in space, not time," she said.

"How do they tell them apart—I mean, things that happened yesterday and things that happened a long time ago?"

"You're missing the point," Carla said.

I propped myself up on one elbow. The moon was almost full; it reflected in the pond. I could see Carla's face, but couldn't tell if she was irritated with me.

"There is no long time ago and no yesterday," Carla said. "They have different classifications for different kinds of events. Like mythological events are on a separate plane maybe from everyday events, in their minds. Not further back on a timeline."

While I was trying to get my head around that, I watched Carla's chest move up and down, a few beads of water shining on her skin, her breasts pushing out to the sides because of how she was lying.

"They see themselves as connected to a place," Carla said, still staring up at the stars. "To the land. A point in space rather than a point in time. It's all part of what they call the dreaming. And it worked fine until the Europeans came along and forced our kind of thinking on them."

I still think about that a lot. I might do better in that kind of culture. It's time that's always kicking my ass. Carla herself was never on time for work, but when she was there it was a whole different place. The second day I worked with her, we were both at the front registers and this woman came up with a bunch of books, put them on the counter in front of Carla and said she wanted to return them. She didn't have her receipt. Our policy was that we could take them back anyway and give her store credit for the cost of them. But Carla just stared at the woman, who started to get nervous and finally said, "Well, can you give me a store credit?"

"I could if you'd bought them," Carla said.

"I just told you I lost my receipt."

"No," Carla corrected, "you just went out and pulled these books off the shelves and now you're pretending you're returning them, which is called stealing."

"That's crazy. Look, I have this bag from your store." She held up the wrinkled plastic bag with our company's logo on it that she'd taken the books out of. "I want to see a manager."

Carla raised her voice, angry. "This store is full of cameras!" she said, waving her arm around over her head like she was getting ready to throw a lasso. "Come on," she said, "I'll show you the tape." She stepped out from behind the counter and nodded toward the back of the store, making like the woman should follow her. "You can meet my manager in back, we'll all review the tape, watch you taking the books off the shelves, putting them in that bag you brought in, and then coming to the counter to return them."

The woman was already backing away, fumbling with the belt on her coat. "No, I'd better—" she said, "I just remembered something." Then she turned and hurried out the door. Carla came back to her register laughing.

"How did you know?" I asked.

Carla shrugged her shoulders. "I didn't."

"I didn't know we had cameras all over this store."

Carla smiled. "Oh, my knight of the crapper," she said. "There aren't any cameras."

Later that same day, we were both stationed at the information counter where Carla was misinforming everybody that the famous cookbook guru had canceled his signing for later that night. "I read somewhere the Nasty is the second fattest city in the country," she told me. "The last thing these people need is to be inspired to cook."

When there was a slow spell, Carla turned to me and said, "Hey, during the next station switch, you wanna run across the street and do a shot?"

There was this bar & grill place across the street. I wasn't sure if she was kidding or not. "Um, I don't think so," I said.

"Me either," she said. "I was just checking. Oh, shit. Here they come, the Batman and Robin of retail."

Rob and Frank, the head manager and the assistant manager were bearing down on us from across the store. I noticed for the first time that, while Rob was taller, with darker hair, he and Frank had matching buzz cuts. They always acted like paramedics at the scene of a disaster.

"Carla, John," Rob said. "Staff meeting in the break room at six." He turned to Frank. "I'll get music, you go to children's."

"Right," said Frank.

"Aye-aye, ten-four," Carla said, doing a military salute as they split.

At six, everybody else was already seated around the table when Carla took the last empty chair directly across from me. She'd let her hair down. It was hanging loose over her shoulders and framed her face in a way that emphasized her cheekbones; she was so striking I had to look down at the faux wood grain of the plastic tabletop. Also, Carla's sweater was thick and real loose, but still you could pretty much tell she wasn't wearing a bra. She pushed up the baggy sleeves and showed smooth tan forearms that had no freckles or anything at all and rested them on the table. You just wanted to touch her all the time, to see if she was actually real.

Rob and Frank were playing nice cop, tough cop. Rob was letting Frank handle the meeting, leaning against the sink, while Frank sat up so straight at the head of the table that he looked way taller than he was. They were all pumped about this book-signing because the cook had a TV show and we had to be ready for millions of hungry Midwesterners invading the store.

"We've also been getting complaints," Frank said. "Customers have said they call and get hung up on. That they don't get the world-class customer service we normally provide."

Carla kicked my leg. Her elbow resting on the table, she raised her finger to point at me and mouthed, "You better stop that."

Frank raised his voice a little. "This is a serious issue," he said. Rob was nodding—a sad Batman agreeing with his Robin. Frank started to direct his speech right at Carla. "Our personnel is the main edge we have on our competitors."

Carla knitted her eyebrows and assumed a serious expression. With her elbows on the table in front of her, she put the fingertips of one hand to the tips of the other and nodded slightly while Frank talked, like this was real interesting stuff.

"Providing world-class customer service is the one and only way we as a company are going to beat the competition," Frank proclaimed. You had to hand it to the guy, he was just seething with customer service. "Is that clear? Carla?"

Studying her fingertip tepee, she considered the question for a long moment while no one spoke. The she said, "Frank, why don't you lick my balls?"

4

Today I notice that Virginia, who, rumor has it, used to be in theater—whatever that means, exactly—is wearing a red sequin dress when her daughter, a tired-looking housewife, drops her off at daycare. The daughter was really embarrassed, had to keep telling me she couldn't get Virginia to change into something else. Like I give a shit. All I see is that Virginia is happier than usual. During choir practice, she smiles at an imaginary audience, sways to the music and sings a little louder than maybe she ought to.

I'm bummed that Joanne is here because now I don't have an excuse to help Beverly in the kitchen. Not only that, but whereas Bev is always wordlessly doing good Samaritan stuff every second of the day, Joanne, a little brown-haired mouse of a woman, is always saying how God said she had to do this or that, and how God came to her in a dream and woke her up and told her the path she had to take. The way she carries on about God you'd think she was talking about this bossy old curmudgeon who lives in her attic. And of course in her monologues Jesus shows up a lot too. From what I understand, if Jesus existed, he wasn't anybody to sing about. If you've ever met any long-haired carpenters you know what I mean. I have yet to come across one who doesn't seem to think he's the son of God. Conceited play-with-their-hair-in-the-mirror motherfuckers who expect you to be impressed when they take off their shirts, and think that during the time they've spent pounding nails they've penetrated into a secret understanding of the workings of the world.

The Heart of It All

Cliff comes up to me during the pre-snack social. He looks like he hasn't slept in a while. "You're not going to believe what's been happening with Mildred," he tells me.

Right now, Mildred is sitting over on the couch with Deidre and they're pretending to knit. They start with a few different colors of yarn and they'll chat for hours, working their needles till they each have a wad of multicolored yarn they tell you is a sweater or a scarf. There's nothing to do but drape it over your shoulder and say, Thank you so much.

"Last Friday night," Cliff says, "I was trying to get her undressed to get her into her nightgown. She kept accusing me of trying to rape her." Cliff tucks the corner of his mouth up in the wrinkles of his cheek, shakes his head and looks over to where Mildred is happily knitting away.

"We've been married for forty-seven years," he says. "And in five years we haven't more than given each other a peck good night. It's hard to see her like this. She gets so hysterical—she'll scream and throw things at me. Last night I went out to get some groceries and run a few other errands and when I come home the door is locked. I knock and ring the bell and when she comes to the door she won't open it. She kept telling me to go away or she was going to call the cops. She had no idea who I was. And I could see how frightened she was of me. I was standing there with grocery bags in my arms. It was terrible."

"What'd you do?" I ask.

"I pretended to leave—I remembered how you always say to go along with their reality, John." Cliff gives me a nod of thanks, even though I never exactly said that; maybe he's thinking of somebody from his support group for caregivers. "And then I had to climb in through a window on the porch after she'd gone upstairs. She was a little startled when she saw me, but she'd calmed down. Apparently she'd forgotten all about not letting me in the door.

"I don't know how much more I'm going to be able to do on my own. I hate the idea of it, but pretty soon it's going to get where she has to be somewhere she can be properly attended to. I'm getting awfully tired."

It's clear Mildred's condition is deteriorating quickly, and my ignorant, off-the-cuff advice isn't going to help Cliff that much. I wonder if maybe he never wanted my advice before. Maybe it's the other way around; maybe he's been trying to help me.

"You should come to our support group," he tells me.

And it would be an insult to him and his wife for me to try to explain that, in a way, this is my support group. That I've been thinking of Alzheimer's as this sort of aboriginal alternative lifestyle. But I honestly do like it here in the daycare center. People with Alzheimer's have no memory of the past (except long past) and no anxiety about the future. In other words, it's perfect. People like this are way more pleasant to talk to because there isn't pressure from the past and the future squeezing all the life out of the present. Only the moment matters.

Beverly comes out of the kitchen with a tray full of cookies, making that swishing sound—the stockings rubbing together between her thighs as she walks. She has some serious thunder thighs under that bright red and yellow floral print dress she's wearing. I immediately get a lump in my throat. Good God, I'd fuck her silly. All it takes is a swish of thighs, a whiff of that powdery old-ladyish perfume she wears and I'd do anything. I'd go to church with her every single day of the week, if she'd agree that after service, after everybody had smiled at the priest and filed out the door, I could bend her big ass over the altar and bang her brains out. When this hideous horniness takes me over it's like being in a car and having the accelerator get stuck to the floor just when the steering gives out.

Everyone begins to move toward the table where Bev is placing the cookies. I have to imagine eighty-five year old Virginia without her fancy dress on to keep my hard-on down. Joanne scampers out of the kitchen with the juice and passes cups around. Beatrice takes a seat next to Phil, who, I'm noticing for the first time, looks a little like Grandpa Stanley. Same long, rickety frame and trowel chin. Beatrice glances at him as she sits down and smoothes her hair, pats the bun in back. Phil stares straight into space like he's hypnotized. It's really something. This place is practically vibrating with twisted affection.

Phil raises a cup to his mouth, his hand so shaky it almost spills. For whatever reason, he decides to chug-a-lug his entire cup of juice. His head tips back slowly and his Adam's apple bobs once, but then he seems to forget to swallow a second time as his mouth fills up again. He chokes loudly and spews out the juice in a big plume of mist over the table.

"Oh dear, oh dear," Beatrice says, chuckling. She takes a couple napkins and wipes his face, his shirt, and mops around his place at the table. Grace, who has puffy white hair, touches her cheek with her fingertips. Then she looks up at the ceiling and holds out her hand, palm up.

"How did you think we sounded this morning, John?" Beverly asks. "Better than the last time you were with us?"

"Yeah, I'd say so," I say, and try to think of something more encouraging. But the truth is they sounded the same as the first time I ever heard them practice. And today I wasn't really listening. I was looking at the way Beverly's hips went out from her waist and curved down to the piano bench so that, from behind, her upper body looked like a big juicy pear.

"The hospital postponed again so we have an extra week to practice," she says. "But I really think it's important for this first recital to go well for us." She's looking over the group of cookie-nibbling Alzheimer's victims she's including herself in. "It will increase our confidence and the next one will be easier." Her hope for this hopeless crowd makes her round face so tender I want to go down on one knee and kiss the back of her plump white hand.

"Well, Beatrice seems to be looking forward to it," I lie. Beatrice doesn't look forward to anything, as far as I can tell, but sometimes at home I'll hear her humming one of the tunes they practiced here.

"Really?" Beverly says, brightening up. Her blue eyes get more spectacular. So do other things. Until I met Beverly, I never noticed before how a woman's double chin can be kind of sexy.

"Because that's what I've been hoping," Bev says. "That it can help us start to make the connection to time that's been disturbed. As a group, we'll have things to look forward to, and then to look back on. It could help."

Oh, she is so sweet I could just sacrifice my life for this woman. I want to rush over and start tickling her. I'm about to say something about how I want to help the cause, even though I hate memory, when Joanne butts in.

"Because we're all God's children and we have to help one another along," she tacks on, like it's the logical caboose to Beverly's train of thought. Joanne has a real whiny, monotonous voice. "We never know what His plans may be, but I know I beg his forgiveness and mercy every day and every night. I've been praying for Him to see us through the recital."

"I think God sucks," I want to say. It's all I can think, so I don't say anything. Neither does Beverly; she just smiles. But I bet if you pressed her (and how I'd love to press her!) she'd admit Joanne goes a little overboard with the self-righteous Godspeak. But, she'd remind you, Joanne is doing good work and her heart is in the right place. Is Beverly's problem that she's too generous? Is that something it's possible to be? All I know is I'm not the selfless saint she is, and I'm not even half the good person she thinks I am for bringing Beatrice here. I'm doing it for my own reasons. I don't know where my heart is or what the right place for it is.

Beatrice gets up from the table with Phil, takes his arm to help him as he shuffles over to a chair by the window, and I decide I'm going to help her regain some memory, or at least try to stop her from getting worse. Just being there for somebody isn't enough.

So how's this for a business idea: you buy a big piece of land way far away from the city where it's cheap as crap, mow down all the trees, every last stick, and haul them out. You take all the topsoil out while you're at it. Make the trees into woodchips. Make floppy boards out of the woodchips and make big flimsy houses out of the boards. Sell these houses to people where they can live on the desert you've created far from the Nasty ghetto. Then you sell them back the topsoil so they have something to put around the houses that will grow grass on it so they can have something to mow. Since there are no trees, you sell them a few overpriced saplings and shrubs to put around their woodchip houses. And since you still have woodchips left over, you convince folks what they need is mulch. Because it wouldn't be worth having—I mean, it couldn't hardly even count as a tree if it didn't have a ring of mulch around it to highlight it and let the neighbors know, "Hey, look here, I paid good money for this—it's a tree!" Or a caricature of one anyways, since right where it is there used to be a real, four-hundred-year-old tree so big that when we looked at it we couldn't comprehend the whole thing so what we had to do was break it down into smaller pieces we could understand. Like fucking woodchips. Okay, so to make the mulch you take some of the sewage being pumped out of the houses you built, soak your wood chips in it with some other chemicals and some dye so it keeps that natural rich brown color. So these folks are buying back their own shit and little pieces of their own trees at the same time! Ha, ha, ha!

Just kidding—that's not a business idea at all. It's just good, plain, commonsense capitalism. Yeehaw! Gotta luv it, gotta luv it. Because if you don't you're nothing but goddamn negative asshole creep! You're un-American! Because these here is nothing but honest, hard-working, god-fearing earth salts, who would kindly like to live out here on the surface of the moon where their kids can go to school without getting stabbed or shot by a—well, they ain't prejudiced or nothing—but nonetheless.

So where we at Ryan Rinckel, Inc. come in, is at the end, to put the icing on the subdivision. "The amigos won't be here for another couple weeks," Ryan tells me. As usual, he sounds like he's talking out his nose. "So you'll be going out with Terry's crew for now."

I can't get over the hairpiece. The problem is, it forces you to be an accomplice in this lie. It's like when girls wear those tiny tank tops and underneath it they have those booby-trap bras that smash them together and push them up out of the tank top and into your face. And then they mean to stand there and talk to you—but don't look down, you pervert! The nerve! I imagine Ryan in a bar trying to pick up a girl like that. Them both trying to talk to each other without looking at each other's lies. How depressing.

I go out to the pit and help unload the tools from the truck so Terry can load it up with mulch. Then we put all the tools back on the truck because Ryan is too cheap to invest in tool boxes that could be welded right on underneath the truck bed.

Terry is one of these tough, potato-famine Irish guys you meet in every blue collar job you ever get. He seems to have more muscles in his forearms than other people. You can easily picture legions of him building railroads across this country and leading platoons through jungles to fight our wars.

There are four of us in this mildew-scented cab and it's a long haul from the ghetto our customers have abandoned to their subdivision north of the Nasty where we've got to take this mulch. As we merge on to 71, Terry says, more to Joe than me or Wade, "You know, I was thinkin'."

"Oh shit, not again," says Joe. You can see these two have been working together a while. I get the feeling they're used to sparking up about now, but aren't, because Wade and I are new.

"Shut up motherfucker," Terry says. "They had this thing on TV last night about how many motherfuckers they got in India." I've already spent enough time with him this morning to know that by motherfuckers Terry means human beings. "Guess how many there is."

"I thought they was all here by now," says Joe. "They're all over my fucking neighborhood."

"A billion," says Terry. "Now you stop to think, there's so many motherfuckers on this planet, if you died it wouldn't make no difference." As he flicks his lighter to light a cigarette, the muscles ripple under the skin of his freckled forearms.

"No," Joe says. "You mean if *you* died it wouldn't make no difference. It'd matter if I died." Joe is half hillbilly and half ghetto boy, a hybrid you only find in redneck cities like the Nasty. He likes to pace around and wave his arms when he talks, but since right now he's wedged in here between Wade and me, he just rocks back and forth, which reminds me of Phil, who sits doing this sometimes for an hour at the daycare center.

"What the fuck difference would it make if you died?" Terry asks, flicking his ashes out the window, which he's got wide open while the heat is on full blast. "Look at all these motherfuckers," he lifts his freckled hand from the wheel to gesture at the first trickle of morning traffic around us.

I'm sure glad Ryan started hiring stoners instead of drunks. He must be serious about staying off the sauce. Used to be, in the mornings everybody was hung over and wouldn't do anything but grunt till after lunchtime. Interstate 71, I notice, has a lot of billboards with ads for computers, cell phones and cars. With unfinished slogans and blank spaces waiting to be filled.

The subdivision we're working in is an older one where the developers were shortsighted enough to leave an awful lot of the original trees standing. We're doing a clean-up. Left to itself, the land will invariably make a mess, so it's only natural that you have to hire landscapers.

It's a cool, crisp morning with a sky so blue you want to stand there staring at it, trying to judge how far you're seeing. And quiet except for a few birds. Then we bring the blowers roaring to life and obliterate the whole morning chasing leaves out of the beds of groundcover. The air would be nice if I didn't have to breathe carbon dioxide from the shrieking two-cycle engine on my back, which puts out as much exhaust as about four cars and makes you deaf at the same time. I keep having to raise the cuff of my flannel to wipe the drop of liquid that the cool air makes run out and dangle from the tip of my nose. I'll be doing the same thing in a couple months, except on the sleeve of a t-shirt, because it'll be so hot and the drop of moisture will be the sweat that's always running down the top of my nose. But it's good to be outdoors. The great outdoors! Even if it is just somebody's back yard.

By lunch, my shoulder muscles have knots in them from the straps holding the blower on. Terry and Joe ask us if we want anything at the store before they go off in the truck to burn a joint someplace while Wade and I sit and eat our lunches on the grass. Takes him no time to launch into a list of the reasons his ex-wife is an evil witch who despises the males of our species. Out of all the poor slobs in the tri-state area, she had to pick Wade's sorry ass to torture for a lifetime and make an example of. It's hard not to feel bad for him, the grown-up version of the fat kid alone at the end of the lunch table. No wonder he's got an ax to grind with the whole world. Nobody ever wants to talk to him and here he is now with his five days of stubble, his belly pressing out his shirt, alimony payments pressing on his mind. Even though he's just dumping on me, if there was something I could do for him, it'd be done in a second. While he's talking, I lie back on the grass and drop my extra flannel over my face.

The Heart of It All

Wade's been working on that gut of his for every one of his forty-odd years. So when he has to push it, plus a wheelbarrow of mulch, up the slight rise in the back yard that afternoon, he makes sure and let me know how hard it is, saying, Whew, oh my God. He keeps stopping, trying to get me to talk so he can take a break. Terry stands up on the hill of mulch in the truck bed and pitch-forks it—ferociously, and most of the time with a cigarette in the corner of his mouth—into our wheelbarrows. You can see how he got those forearms. We sling the mulch around in the beds we've blown out. To me, what mulch smells like is used chewing tobacco; it brings up memories of doing this same crap all those years ago. After a while it just gets to be the smell of work.

Ryan stops by in the afternoon to police us. He gives me a stack of green shirts with his name and logo on it, and a pair of new pruners. "Welcome back to the team," he says. It's an expensive watch he's wearing—heavy, gold, with all kinds of little dials but no numbers. One of those things you look at and can't ever figure out what time it is. He turns to the other guys as he slaps my shoulder. "Have I told you guys what a fortitudular worker this guy is? He's smart too. Don't underestimate this one."

I know he's only saying this bullshit to make me feel good, reasoning that this will keep me working hard for him. But even though, it makes me feel good. He starts to drive off in his shiny white truck with his name and leaf on the door without giving Wade any shirts. Which makes me embarrassed. Ryan stops all the sudden and yells out the window at Terry to put up one of his signs. Terry gets one of the foam board signs that has the Ryan Rinckel, Inc. leaf on it out of the truck and sticks it in the yard. Then after Ryan's truck is out of sight, he kicks it over. It occurs to me that Ryan should have said it out loud to himself before he added the "Inc." to his name. Because it's almost like naming your company Rinky-Dink.

It heats up in the afternoon, so we're all smelling pretty ripe by the time we have to squeeze back in the truck for the ride back to the shop. Terry's in a philosophical mood again. He turns the radio down. "I was listening to this thing on the radio the other day, they was talking about if you died tomorrow, what's the one thing you'd want motherfuckers to remember you for."

"My pruning," I say.

Terry lights a fresh cigarette with the end of his last one and throws the old butt out the window as traffic slows to almost a stop. The creases on his knuckles are brown from the mulch. Because the truck rides high, we can see over the vehicles ahead of us to where there are a couple cars pulled over and some people are standing around, probably discussing a fender-bender. The wheel might save Terry, but if we get in an accident, the other three of us are going right through the windshield. All four of us have cigarettes going and since the traffic stopped, cutting off the breeze through our open windows, there's so much smoke it's like we started a campfire in here.

"I wanna go live on a desert island," Terry says.

Joe bobs forward in his seat to say, "Why a desert island?"

"Yeah," I say, "why not a tropical island with a forest?"

"Nah, nah," Terry grimaces and waves his hand. "'Cause then there'd be all them birds and shit makin' noise."

Next morning we're loading up the trucks. Not even for physical reasons, just as part of his general drone, Wade starts to complain about getting old. I'm sorry, but it always seems to me that the people who complain about aging aren't doing much else. I never in my life heard Beatrice complain about getting old.

Then this other foreman starts bossing me around the pit. While he's sitting on the Bobcat, he yells at me to put a tarp over the mulch on his truck, so he can dump a couple yards of manure on it. I climb up and do it, then get back down and start over to Terry's truck to see what he needs, but this other guy tells me to start loading up his tools with Wade.

I tell him I'm on Terry's crew and he says he doesn't care.

Today, Wade has been moved to this other guy's crew, so when Terry, Joe and I are riding out to our job, we have some elbow room. "So you worked here a few years ago?" Terry asks me. Turns out he started with Ryan less than a year after I left town. I can see what he and Joe are wondering, so I tell them how once, back in the old days, I got so stoned and drunk with Ryan at a work party that Ryan passed out right on his own front lawn with his wife screaming at him, and he didn't get up till the next morning. This gives Terry his opening to ask if I still get high, and I say yeah. So then everything's much more comfortable among the three of us and the conversation just rolls right along while Joe rolls a joint.

You probably wouldn't believe it by now, but I really don't get high. Or not much. But you can hardly avoid it half the time. Society demands sacrifice. Like if somebody offers you a cigarette in prison, you're not about to say, "Oh, no, thank you old chap. I don't smoke. I'm concerned about my health, you see." Might as well tape a sign to your own back that says, "Nice, tight asshole."

I ask about the other foreman. "Jim, he just started," Terry says. "Why, he bustin' your balls already?"

"Kind of bossy isn't he?"

"He just graduated. He got an associate degree in landscaping. Ryan's head over heels in love with the motherfucker."

"Degree?" I say, taking the joint from Joe. "Who the hell goes to school to learn about this shit?"

"A turd burglar," Joe answers, jovially. "Did you see him today? Dude's got this fancy briefcase he keeps contracts in. I wouldn't be surprised if he irons his t-shirts to come out here and sling mulch and shit."

"You'll never see that motherfucker touch mulch with anything but a Bobcat," Terry says. "He has his crew do it all while he stands around and prunes shit."

"They must really love him," I say.

Terry shrugs. "Don't bother him. Him and Ryan are like a couple a dogs with their noses in each other's assholes."

For some reason, it's always way more fun to destroy things than make them nice. So this planting we're starting today is great, because the owners want to rip out these huge taxus bushes in the front of their property by the sidewalk. I pull the rope on a chainsaw and tear a big hole in the suburban silence. My arms are cramped, veins bulging, nose running. Stoned off my ass, wasting these perfectly healthy bushes that these rich people are so tired of looking at. Yes sir, I'm just happy to be a part of the food chain, thanks, though I am pretty far down on it, kneeling here in the dirt as I am with the mites and earthworms and whatnot. But still, I am a certified member of the American workforce!

We loop a chain from the truck chassis to the stump of a taxus and back up real fast to yank it out of the ground. There're about a dozen of them. This is big fun. Joe's behind the wheel and he says he loves this song and turns the radio all the way up. Loud, heavy metal morning.

I'm putting the chain around the sixth one and yelling at Joe to let me have a turn in the truck when she comes out. I can't hear anything because of the music and Terry's still running a chain saw. I don't notice her at first, then there's a white blur in the corner of my eye waving an arm from the corner of the yard. She's probably saying excuse me, but it sounds like "Wee-wee!"

I go over and say hi. She's freshly showered, blown dry, and has the collar of her polo shirt turned up. She wants to know if Ryan is here. Joe has finally seen her, turned the music down and stopped gunning the engine. "I spoke with Ryan this morning," she says. "I was having second thoughts about taking out those bushes."

I look over to where Terry has just finished severing the last one. They're all lying in pieces like gigantic busted tumbleweeds on the lawn and sidewalk. There are little craters with ripped-out stumps everywhere. "I don't think we're going to be able to put them back," I say.

Terry comes over. Says he didn't hear anything from Ryan about a change of plans. He tries to get Ryan on his walkie-talkie. The woman folds her arms and looks around biting her lip. Instead of worried, she looks like this is something she practiced in the mirror.

Terry can't get hold of Ryan. "Last I heard, we were gonna eighty-six the taxus and put viburnum along the front," Terry says.

"Well, now that you've gone ahead and taken those out, I'm not so sure viburnum is what would look best there. I was thinking maybe a hedge of burning bush instead." We all stand there looking at her devastated front yard. Joe is smoking a cigarette in the truck with the music just barely audible. "Well what do you think?" she says, in a tone that implies we've been arguing with her. "I mean, you're the landscapers," she says.

"Well, it's your land," I say. "What do you want it to look like?" Then she stares at me like I've got boogers all over my face.

"Burning bush would probably look good there," Terry says, taking the radio off his belt again. "Lemme try again and see if I can get Ryan."

I stare right back at the lady till she looks away. I'm not so stoned I can't recognize low-rent royalty when I see it. They're the same ones who want special treatment in retail stores. What they really want are servants, like butlers, maids and a gardener. But they can't afford it, so they hire landscapers and nannies so they can get that feeling of being perpetually waited-on, but they hound the help all day so they can also feel like they're get their money's worth. This woman is pretending to want our opinion so she can contradict it. Terry and I, since we don't even own Rincky-Dink Landscaping, are too far down the social ladder for her to even really discuss with us something as important as a decision about her hedge.

Carla could spot low-rent royalty a mile away. When they came to the info counter and asked for a book, they expected us to go find it on the shelves for them and put it in their hands, which according to corporate policy, we were supposed to do. Carla would just stand there and say, "Yeah, that shouldn't be hard to find. It's a novel, so maybe you should go look in the fiction section."

Like I guessed would probably happen, Ryan shows up soon and this housewife spends the entire morning leading him and Terry all around her property, stopping to pose with her face cupped thoughtfully in her hand, pointing at different plants and flower beds on her property. She gets Terry so pissed that by the end of the day, driving back to the shop, he cuts off some guy driving a mid-life-crisis-mobile—one of those convertible sports cars that looks like they were trying to make the shape of the body as close to a woman's as they could get it. At the next light, the guy pulls up next to us and yells at Terry to watch where the hell he's going. Terry leans out of the truck, a vein bulging out of his neck as he lets the nice man know, loud and clear, that he has Terry's permission to go fornicate with himself.

I promise myself I'm going to make good on my resolution to do good this weekend. Beverly inspired me to make this resolution. Even though I don't want my own, I'm going to help Beatrice exercise her memory, because I've read that doing this could slow the Alzheimer's. But it's still only Friday night and I have all those billboards to take care of. I slide into Gary's car with my gear. You can tell what he does for a living without him saying anything.

"It smells like a large pepperoni in here," I say.

"Keep your snout outta my crotch," Gary says. "It bothers you so much, we can take your car."

"My grandmother's," I say. "I don't think we'd better." The thing is, I don't quite have an exactly valid driver's license at the moment, and I know from experience you're more likely to be pulled over in the wee hours. I give Gary some gas money.

The billboards I want to hit on 71 are on even higher poles than the ones on 75. So I have to spend even more time shakily climbing up and down. The first thing I want to write goes on a billboard telling people to donate their old cars to a church charity. There's the huge fat face of Father O'Malley, under which I write, GOD SUCKS.

Another billboard advertises a shopping mall. It shows two young couples with brilliantly white teeth laughing and pulling at each other's new sweaters like a bunch of retards. Beneath them, I write, SWEATSHOPPERS. On a cigarette billboard where a cowboy is chasing cattle, I get ballsy and spend the time to write, SELL CANCER TO THE TURD WORLD. On a vodka billboard, DILUTE YOUR MEANINGLESSNESS. On one for a fast food restaurant, EAT CHEMICALS. The way I look at it, this is just the flip side of my landscaping. I slip from working in the service industry to working in the disservice of industry. I'm only doing it for the benefit of these drones who'll see it. I spend the day, exposed by light, covering up the ugly truth of their world with mulch, sod and ornamental trees. Then I spend the night, under cover of darkness, exposing the ugly truth beneath the surface of their lives. Yet I'm invisible to them the whole time.

I don't wake up till noon Saturday morning. The room I sleep in is the one I used when I came to visit as a little kid. I told Beatrice I wanted to be one of the Pixies and so all over the walls she painted trees that rise up into a blue sky that gets darker as it goes toward the center of the ceiling where it's all black, but speckled with yellow stars and planets. There are Pixies climbing in and out of holes in the trees, peeking out at you from behind leaves, and doing cartwheels on the grass. On the ocean that takes up one wall is a scene from my favorite of the books, where the Pixies are on a ship, climbing and dangling all over the rigging, clinging from the side rails, several of them trying not very successfully to handle the steering wheel.

I get out of bed and head down to the kitchen, but at the bottom of the stairs, I hear Beatrice talking. I stop. Maylene must be here. They're in the kitchen.

"Oh no, you've done a fine job this year," Beatrice says. There's no response. Then Beatrice says, "Well yes, I understand, but I'd like to get them out by the end of the month."

There's no phone in the kitchen. I tiptoe over to the front window—no car except Beatrice's. A spoon clinks in a bowl and Beatrice sighs. "Okay, okay, we can do it that way, I suppose," she says.

When I walk in the kitchen I startle her. She looks confused for a second, but covers it up right quick with a smile. "Well, good morning dear," she says. She's eating a bowl of oatmeal. She usually gets up at five, so this could be a second breakfast. Sometimes by the time she's washed the breakfast dishes she'll have forgotten she ate and start making breakfast again. Then she doesn't eat the second one because she's full. I help myself to some oatmeal because she's made enough for a family, then I sit down across the table from her.

"Hadn't you better hurry?" she says. "Won't you be late for school?"

So I'm my father today; at least for now. "There's no school today," I say.

"Oh, that's right," she says.

Over her shoulder I notice a movement. Something is dripping from one of the cabinets. Beatrice looks out the back window. "I was thinking what a nice day it is to be outside anyway," she says.

"We should go for a walk," I say. She seems to think this is a good idea, and gets up as soon as I put my bowl in the sink. She's all ready to go for a walk in her bedroom slippers till I suggest she change into her brown shoes instead. I decide to let her stay in the powder blue nightgown because I don't want to have to go through the tedium and embarrassment of keeping her on track while she's changing, which otherwise would take forever. While she's tying her shoes, I open the cabinet where the plates and bowls are stacked and find it's a half-gallon of vanilla ice cream that's dripping onto the counter. I toss it out and clean up the white puddles in the cabinet and on the counter.

We walk slow, arm-in-arm on the path that skirts the field, goes behind the leaning barn, through a patch of woods and down to the pond. As we're walking, Beatrice seems to be perking up. She says my name at one point, which is unusual. The pond is not the big Loch Ness of my childhood imagination, but still it's a good-sized, spring-fed pond, and some people around here would consider it a lake. The rope swing is still here, dangling over the water from its limb, but the tire that used to be on it is gone.

Once upon a time, Carla's naked body rose out of this body of water. She shook her hair back and wrung the water out of it as she came walking up onto the bank. She was so instantly comfortable here it seemed like she belonged to the place, or it belonged to her. As the summer went on, her skin got browner, her hair a little wilder, decorated with lighter streaks. She sat right here on this flattened grassy little bank that's like a platform a few inches above the surface of the pond. With her feet dangling down in the water, she bent forward with her chin resting on her palms, her elbows on her knees. She was like a nymph fresh out of the forest for her daily bath.

Does life have to keep going on, leaving empty stage sets like this all over the place? You try to seize the day, but it seems to be made of mercury. Beautiful, but it keeps slipping through your fingers. You can't ever get it together.

Beatrice is leaning more heavily on my arm, even panting a little. She didn't get a whole lot of exercise even when she was well. There's a log Carla and I used to throw our clothes on. I tell Beatrice we can sit here and rest for a while.

"This place," she says. "You loved this place so."

"Still do," I say.

"Your father never cared for it so much," she says.

Wait a minute, I think. "You remember me—I mean what I was like then?"

She pats my knee. "You think I'd forget my only grandson?"

I could fall backward off the log. Sometimes I wonder if she's been just doing an act and she's going to hang it up one day and go back to being her old self.

"It was so wonderful to have you and your friends come down here," she says. She looks down and smoothes her nightgown along her knee. "Especially after Stanley was gone," she says. "You kept this place alive." She looks up at me and smiles, the darker skin around her moist eyes going all crinkly.

"I still miss Carla," I say, surprising myself a little with the confession. What I'd wanted was to provide some solidarity. And it would have been a lie to say I missed grumpy grandpa Stanley.

"I know," Beatrice says. "Oh what a wildcat, that one. Really—a force of nature." She seems to stop herself, realizing that this isn't cheering me up. She moves her hand from her knee to mine and gives it a little pat. The tips of the index and middle fingers of her wrinkled little hands are crooked, bending away after the last joint, making her hands look like old gloves that got wet and dried funny. On anyone younger, you'd think these fingers were broken. I wonder what happens.

"It gets easier," Beatrice says, looking out at the water. "There are different people for different seasons. You learn to appreciate that."

"Really?"

"Would I sit here and lie to my only grandson?" After a pause she says, "And you have to think about how you've preserved things. The waters get muddied. You have a perfect picture of something you couldn't see the flaws in at the time and the things you think were horrible might have had some good in them. I drew some wrong."

The Heart of It All

Beatrice has gotten a look on her face like she's working out some problem of perspective, which I'd watched her do many times, years ago, with a sketch pad in front of her. I'm afraid she might have wandered from this clearing we seemed to be in, down a side path, back into some overgrown thicket in her mind. I remember my resolution about trying to improve her memory.

"Come on," I say, standing up and holding my hand out. "Let's walk a little more and then do a little project." What I have in mind is a memory strength drill I thought up. Since the brain is a muscle, I figure you've got to be able to do exercises to strengthen parts that are getting weak. Beatrice places her hand in mine and gives me one of those sweet little smiles that she does mostly with her eyes, keeping her lips pressed shut. Like I just asked her to dance and she knows a pretty funny secret about me.

When we get back to the house, I go up in the attic and rummage around until I find photo albums and a big box of letters I bring down to the living room. I go collect copies of all the Pixies books from where they're scattered on bookshelves in different rooms and bring them in too. On the couch next to Beatrice, I unfold a photo album and point to a picture of my parents on their wedding day. They look like kids playing dress-up. I realize I'm seven years older than they were in that picture.

"Who's that?" I ask.

"Why that's George and his wife Elizabeth," Beatrice says.

I flip through the album. "And that?" I ask, pointing to a picture of Sheila after a soccer game with her arms around her teammates, dirt and grass stains all over their uniforms.

Beatrice shifts her legs under the photo album. "That's Maylene's daughter," she says, a little irritated she can't remember the name.

I show her a ten-year-old picture of myself. She looks at me like I've lost all my marbles. "Now don't tell me you can't recognize yourself," she says. "Honestly, Jonathan, you like to play some awfully silly games."

I come to a picture of someone I'd totally forgotten. I point at it. "Hey, remember Dave the duck?" I say, before I remember I'm supposed to ask her the name, which is the main part—well actually so far the only part I've thought of—of this training.

"Oh yes," Beatrice says. "What a terrible identity jigsaw he had."

Dave thought he was a dog. He slept in the doghouse with the two other dogs. He chased cars down the driveway and imagined he was barking when he quacked at strangers. If you picked him up and threw him in the pond Dave would get all pissed-off, flapping and quacking like he was on fire, and he'd paddle right back out again and try to shake himself off the way a dog does. Then he'd quack-bark at you a few times, waddle off down the path to go spend the next hour or so sulking in the doghouse.

I leave the photo album on Beatrice's lap and start rooting through a box full of old letters, hoping to find ones from friends and relatives with dates on them to get her oriented in the right time. There are a lot that have the letterhead of the company that published the Pixies books. I keep ignoring these till I start to notice they're all addressed to Beatrice. Not Stanley. Some just say stuff like, "Enclosed please find the final proofs and blah, blah, blah." Then I glance at the middle of one from 1952 that says, "I hope you can work this out without sacrificing the rhyme. Our wording is of course merely a suggestion." Of course. But it's addressed to Beatrice. This can't be right. What everyone always said, and the reason his name was bigger than hers on the cover, was that Stanley wrote the books and did the majority of the illustrating; Beatrice only helped with adding a few Pixies here and there. On most of them it says, "By Stanley Ritter," and underneath that, in type less than half the size, "With Beatrice Ritter." She wouldn't have had time to do all this work, what with raising the kids and making all the meals. There's another letter from the same editor to Beatrice with a date of 1960. It says, "I understand your concern, and Stanley's name may appear on the cover as usual. But we cannot accept any more of his drawings. The quality simply does not match up."

I put the letter on top of the photo album Beatrice is looking through. "What's this all about?" I ask.

Beatrice looks it over and makes several little kissing sounds by clicking the tip of her tongue on the roof of her mouth. She passes it back to me. "I wish you'd put this away. We don't want something like that left around, now do we? He'd have a flying conniption." Then she loses interest and goes back to the photo album. "Certainly would," she mumbles to herself. "Certainly, certainly."

"Wait," I say. "You mean to tell me grandpa didn't even draw anything for some of these books?" I stick my open hand out at the stack of Pixies picture books I'd put next to her on the couch.

Beatrice smiles so her cheeks bulge up like smooth pink little islands with wrinkles lapping all around them. "Between you and me, he wasn't very good," she says. "And so slow! Ugh!"

Now I'm remembering something Carla said. It was after one of the first times she met Beatrice and Stanley, and we were driving back from the farm to my place. We'd been having a fight about something before we got to the farm, had turned it off for while we were there, but now it was back on again and a few sharp words between us had brought back an uncomfortable silence. To break it up, I said something about Stanley writing all those Pixies books, because I knew Carla loved them as much as I did.

"You really think he wrote them?" she said.

"Why not?" I said.

She blew a puff of air between her lips that dismissed the idea and pushed a strand of hair away from her face. "Try talking to the two of them for about five minutes."

Then, because Carla went on a tirade about men taking credit for every goddamn thing under the sun, while women do all the work, at the time, I just thought, Well, what does she know.

"Show me which ones he drew," I say now, putting one of the Pixies books on Beatrice's lap.

She leafs through it till she comes to a picture that takes up a whole page. It's the one where the Pixies borrow a horse and wagon on Halloween night because they want to go on a hayride. The poor tired old horse is plodding along with about twenty Pixies—dressed up as vampires, pirates and skeletons—working the reins, swarming all over his bridle, dangling from spokes on the wheels and falling off the bales of hay on the wagon.

"See here?" Beatrice adjusts her glasses and points to a group of Pixies who've fallen off and are running to catch up with the wagon. "You can tell his by the ears and noses."

The Pixies' noses are little nubs that stick out and turn up slightly at the end like Beatrice's. Their ears stick out between the leaves of their caps; they're elongated and come to points at the top. But these particular Pixies chasing the wagon have shorter ears and longer noses that are just this side of a troll's. And everything about this group is shaky and tentative—they're not made of the bold slashes and loops that make the Pixies so dynamic and spontaneous.

I point this out to Beatrice and she says, "I know. He started to lose his line altogether." She shakes her head at the slightly deformed Pixies trying to get back on the wagon. "He liked to drink, you know," she says.

Then I remember something else from when I was little. Stanley pottering around in the garden all day while Beatrice was in the studio. And it was almost always grandpa who went down to the pond to keep an eye on me in the humid, hazy afternoons. While I swam, he sat on a stump, steadily smoking the unfiltered cigarettes that finally killed him.

"Then you're the real creator of the Pixies," I say to Beatrice, who's looking through one of her own books, smiling at the capers of the creatures she invented like she's seeing them for the first time.

"Oh, now I wouldn't say that," she says. "It all belonged to Stanley. I just helped, really."

"You just said yourself he wasn't very good."

"Who?"

"You. I mean Grandpa. He wasn't really a good artist."

"No, Stanley was a great artist. Not all artists can draw perfectly. He designed. It was our life. Some things you don't know about pumpernickels. It all gets in the sauce."

Now I'm all mixed up and so I take refuge in one of the Pixies books, flipping through, skimming the words and examining the much more fun, upside down world of the Pixies. And then it hits me, what I'm supposed to do with my life. It's not like the time I was living in a cramped room in a big city watching a nature program on TV and I did a speedball and decided I should be a forest ranger. It's not anything like that at all. I know for sure I belong right here making Pixies books in the same studio my grandmother made the first ones in. That's it. I make a new world based on the old one. And then I live in it.

I'm so excited I'm trembling when I go into the studio in back and clear off all the crap, like blouses and old bras that have accumulated on Beatrice's drafting board, and get out some paper. I look out at the overgrown field—I'm going to cultivate that, I decide, when I need a break from drawing award-winning children's books. Is Carla ever going to flip-out when she picks up one of the new Pixies books in a bookstore and sees "By John Ritter" under the title.

The first one will be about this knight who tries to round up all the Pixies and get them to fight the forces of evil, only he doesn't know what to do and ends up leading them on all kinds of wild-goose chases. Carla will be the only one who gets it: why this knight wears a toilet plunger on his head.

I find out real fast it's easier to imagine all that than get anything down on paper that doesn't look like a little kid did it. Beatrice's Pixies wear Robin-Hood-style stockings that droop off their skinny thighs and booty type moccasins that turn up into little curlicues at the toes. My Pixies just look like plump stick figures with broken bones.

I figure that can wait; I'll work on drawing other, simpler, stuff for now. But man, there're a lot of lines in just a rickety old barn or something. I decide maybe I'll do a more modern, streamlined version of the Pixies books so I don't have to draw so much. But then I think about it for a minute. That's stupid. The thing that's so great about the Pixies books is you can feast your eyes on the details of all the dozens of little scenes going on in combination to form one big scene that takes up a whole page. And it's only black and white.

What I need is for Beatrice to give me some pointers. She's not in the living room anymore. Albums, letters and loose photographs are everywhere on the floor like they've been all tossed up in the air at once. I hear the toilet flush upstairs. When I get up there, I hear her talking. This always creeps me out, because it sounds like she's really talking to somebody in particular, somebody she's comfortable with. You expect to hear another voice answer even though you know there's nobody else in the house.

"No, that's no good," Beatrice says. "There you go." I walk in and she's standing there with a jewelry box in one hand, scrabbling around in it with the other. Plop, plop. Two earrings go into the toilet. In those first moments when she sees me come into a room, her expression always makes it seem like she's running around in her mind, picking up pieces and tying up loose ends and trying to get everything back the right way. But it's just like when the Pixies clean up after they've been making pies and cakes in somebody's kitchen all night. They wind up putting the flour in the silverware drawer, sticking the rolling pin and pie pans under the couch cushions.

"Are you sure you want to do that?" I ask Beatrice.

Beatrice looks at the jewelry box and then the toilet, all innocent and guilty like a kid caught raiding the cookie jar. Her eyebrows go up and down. The clouds have rolled back into her head. "I thought," she says, "as long as we were doing all this spring cleaning?"

I pick up the waste basket. "Why don't we throw that stuff out in here," I say. "It'll be easier on the plumbing that way."

"Okay," she says. Seeming relieved, she dumps the rest of the jewelry into the waste basket. I'll have to fish it out of later when she's not looking.

5

I know something's up on Monday morning because everybody's running around loading the trucks in an extra-efficient way. Then Ryan wants to talk to me in the office. He tells me to sit on the other side of the battered desk. In accordance with the new professionalism shtick, he starts out sociable.

"You know, when you first called me up and told me you wanted to work here again, I was real happy," he says. "I thought, now here's a guy I know I can trust, who I know is a good worker. And he knows he can trust me. I was really excited. More than that—I was euphonic."

He pauses. From the pit, I can hear the whine of the Bobcat turning around and the counter-weights on it clanking together. Ryan's smiling at me real hard and it reminds me of something. One of those pictures you see in the paper of a man all the neighbors say they thought was just about the nicest guy in the world till the cops found out he had a bathtub full of severed heads or whatever.

"Remember how I said I want you to feel like this is your company?" he asks. I do. "Well I don't think if it was your company, you'd appreciate it if one of your customers felt she was being mouthed-off at by one of your workers."

So that's what this is all about. Back in the old days, Ryan would have just come up to me, red-faced, jabbing a finger in my chest saying, You stupid good for nothing wise ass son of a bitch you better keep your goddamn mouth shut. That would have been normal. This approach is weird. Makes me nervous.

"Now, granted," Ryan says, "Mrs. Neidhart does have some nubile ideas about how she wants her property to look. But we got to deal with that. It's part of the job."

Just then, Jim, the post-doctoral landscaper, steps in and a smirk crosses his face when he sees I'm getting chewed out. He says excuse me, goes back out and shuts the door. I swear to God, he's exactly like Brad. I'd really like to bash his face in for him. The nickname Jim-dandy pops into my head.

Ryan gets up, so I do too. "So let's just remember it's our company," he says. "I don't wanna have to adumbrate you about how we speak to our customers." In the heat of the moment, I can't think of who it is the new vocabulary he bought reminds me of. "Okay, buddy?" he says, and slaps my shoulder. He says buddy the way you'd say asshole.

We both go out, then I remember I left my pruners in there, so I go back in and the phone is ringing. I pick it up and the pissed-off guy on the line wants to talk to the owner. I say okay and put the phone down, and I'm about to go out and get Ryan. I see him through the bars over the water-stained windows, where Jim is standing in front of him reading something off a leather-covered portfolio thingy. Ryan looks like he's on the verge of taking the boy's cheeks in his hands and kissing him on the mouth.

Let's face it. The number is on the side of the truck. No customer would be calling the warehouse at 7:30 in the morning. The Pixie in me picks the phone back up, squeezes my nose between his thumb and index finger and says, "This is Ryan Rinckel."

The guy on the other end launches into this thing he probably rehearsed all weekend about how he can't stand how this world has got so full of degenerates and he sure doesn't appreciate one of them telling him to go fuck himself. While he rants and raves, I make these little gasping noises into the phone and once in a while go "Mmmm," like I'm chewing a caramel. He wants to know how I can hire these rotten imbeciles who don't even know how to drive and then set them loose in the city behind the wheel of a big truck like that.

Well, I'll tell ya, I say, it sure is hard to get good help these days. It's terrible—don't you start to think I don't know it—but I got to hire these lousy bastards because nobody knows how to do good honest hard work anymore. I ask what he does for a living and it turns out he's an accountant. "See, that's what I mean," I say. Even to me it sounds like somebody holding his nose when I talk. "It's a world full of pencil pushers and button punchers. Everybody's afraid of getting their hands dirty."

He says, Well, it's not quite like that, really. I tell him yeah it is, it's exactly like that. People want to drive fancy cars, but they act like you're a scumbag if you're the guy that fixes them. They want to live in big houses, but they treat you like shit because you help build the things. People want nice plants in their yards, but they'd just assume piss on anybody who'd put them there.

On our way out to the job, Terry says, "Do you think there's more motherfuckers in big cities or in rural areas in this country?"

Joe starts bouncing back and forth in his seat. "You don't know that, dude?" he says. "You ignorant fuck." Joe has a little boy's face with big eyes, straight hair and a haircut that looks like someone put a bowl on his head and cut around it. He gets most of his meals from gas stations. For breakfast this morning, he's having prepackaged ice cream cones, mini donuts, a liter of pop and a few cigarettes.

"See, you don't know neither, do you?" Terry says. "What'd you guess—is most of the population in cities or not?"

"Shit. I'm not tellin' you that dude," Joe says. "If you don't know that, you ain't worth talkin' to in the first place."

Terry throws a lighter across me and it hits Joe in the shoulder. Joe says fuck and throws an empty plastic soda bottle that goes right by

Terry's nose and out the open window.

"Now you gonna start throwin' garbage out the window?" Terry says. "John, which do you think it is. Is there more people in the country or cities?"

I'm twisting around in the seat, trying to get out the envelope I stuck in my back pocket before I jumped in the truck. "Cities," I say.

"See?" Joe says.

"I don't know man," Terry says. "I'm not saying I'm like Mr. Globetrotter John here, but I've drove around to a lotta lotta places. Seems to me there's motherfuckers in every single nook and cranny. I mean, you drive even out in the middle of the fucking desert. There's motherfuckers living there."

"You ain't never been west of Indy, you bitch," says Joe.

By now I got my paycheck out of the envelope. It's way short. "What's this minus a hundred and ten dollars under 'other deductions'?" I ask.

"Well," Terry says, "them t-shirts you're wearin' is twelve dollar apiece. And that pruner and sheath you got on your belt is another fifty bucks. I guess that about does it."

"You're shittin' me."

Terry shakes his head, blows out a stream of smoke. "I shit you not. It's all part of Ryan's new world order. Here, look." Terry squints from the smoke of the cigarette between his lips as he leans forward and feels around under the seat.

Joe laughs. "Dude, it looks like you're trying to pull something out of your ass."

What he comes up with and puts in my hands is a paperback that looks like somebody kicked it under a truck that was moving and then left it buried in a pile of mulch for about a month. *The Seven Habits of Highly Effective People*. "He gave us each a copy," Terry says. "Well, not 'gave,' took the money out of our checks, but he told us to read it at home."

"Problem is, Terry's illiterate," Joe says. "You want John to read it aloud to you?"

"I guess it could be worse," I say. "At least there's only seven of them. I don't think I could memorize any more habits than that. On top of the ones I've already got."

"Look in there and see is smoking one of 'em," Joe says.

I hand Joe the book, look at my check again and do some sloppy remedial math in my head. "It still isn't right," I say.

"He's also not paying for travel time to and from the job," Terry says. "Unless you're a foreman and you're driving the truck."

"What?" I say. "Jesus Christ, no way. Is all this shit even legal?"

Terry shrugs. I start in calling Ryan every nasty name I can think of and even start inventing new ones specially made for him.

"Just be happy if that check even clears, dude," Joe says. "Seems like every week one of us's check bounces. We're stopping at a bank at lunchtime—you don't wanna be the last one to cash your check today. Believe me. Have you seen this shit, dude?" All a sudden he's pointing through the windshield at one of my billboards. "This one up here is the best," Joe says. It's one of Gary's. I pretend I haven't seen it before and Joe and I both laugh.

"What's the matter, Terry, you don't think that's funny?" Joe asks.

"No," he says. "What, I'm s'posed to be happy about that?" He lifts his calloused hand, which is already brown with dirt, from the steering wheel to gesture at the billboard. "Because motherfuckers are spray-painting billboards and shit? Naw, man, that's fucked up."

"Get the fuck outta here," Joe says. But Terry's serious. He's not the kind of guy who will say he doesn't like something just because he's in a bad mood. And it kind of makes me feel crappy that he doesn't like what Gary and I did.

Well, Ryan turned over a new leaf all right. But when a tent worm turns over a new leaf, what he's going to do is gnaw away at it till the whole thing is gone, just like he did last time. All day long while we're finishing Mrs. Neidhart's planting, every time I jam my shovel in the ground I think about sinking it into Ryan's chest, prying open his rib cage, scooping his warm pulsating guts out and flinging them on the grass. Or walking up to him and saying, Hey, if this company is part mine, then part of this shovel is mine, right? And here, I believe this is the part that belongs to you—whapang! That's the business end, Ryan! Right upside your head! Look out for a flying tent worm toupee everybody!

I don't get it when people talk about small businesses being the heart and soul and backbone and fibula and funny bone and spirit of our great nation. In my experience, the smaller the business, the bigger the tightwad, slave-driving, incompetent egomaniac running the show. But I just work here. What do I know? Not a lot. Plenty of people will attest to that.

"So what is this bullshit?" I say to Ryan at the end of the day, after the trucks are put away and everybody else has taken off. He seems ready for me. He just leans back in his chair, lights a cigarette, real calm and professional in his white RR shirt like he never in his life stood in the middle of a parking lot during a Bengals game, pissing on somebody's car. I want him to get riled up and shout back at me like we used to in the good old days.

"You expect me to pay to wear an advertisement for your company?" I say. "And not paying us when we're going out to the job? What the hell?"

"Well, I'm surprised John, I really am," Ryan says, just placid as a mud puddle. "I'd think you'd be happy to have this job," he says. "You know, a lot of employers would prob'ly consider it a favor to take you on after your little escapade in Arizona."

Ah, shit. Well, okay. "There's more than one side to that story," I say.

"Oh hey, I'm sure there is John, I'm sure there is. We all make mistakes. I accept that. But now you got to accept this—as I alluded to before, imagine this is your company. Now I can't afford to be paying all these guys to sit in a truck for forty minutes twice a day," blah, blah, blah. I stop listening. I guess he's got a point. No he doesn't. Either way, I know I'm beat, so I just stand there till I can go. And all while he finishes giving me his spiel, he's wearing that smile that says, Your ass is mine.

Naturally, I forgot all about the music recital till Beverly called the night before it to ask if I could drive. While she's apologizing for having to ask, I picture her holding the phone like a dildo for the ear. I picture her round wrist and soft white hand with dimples on the back where knuckles would be on somebody else. There's probably a cup of tea on the table next to her.

I wish I could be the armchair in Beverly's living room so every night she would settle her nice big round behind down on my lap. Every night, when she first sat down—sproing!—she'd feel that one loose spring pop up with almost enough force to come right through the cushion. "Oh my!" she'd say. A little of the tea would slosh over the rim of the china cup with little flowers and into the saucer in her hand.

Winona is the first one on my list. She gets in the car with not only her usual suitcase, but also a hatbox. Her daughter, who's there to see Winona off, says she's sorry. They couldn't get her to part with her luggage. Winona gets in back, stacks the cases on her lap. That's perfectly okay. Next is Norm, who's wearing an even nicer looking suit than usual, with a red handkerchief neatly folded, sticking out of his breast pocket. Then comes Heidi, a cute little lady who's so wrinkled up she looks like one of those dolls with a peeled, shriveled apple for a head.

Norm starts talking to no one in particular about a new line of products. I glance over my shoulder and see Heidi nodding in agreement with everything he says. Winona is resting her chin on top of her hatbox.

The hospital is in Clifton, not far from all the bars Carla and I used to go to. She must have an unlisted number or else she moved. I can only find her parents' number in the book. I'm sure as hell not going to call them to ask where she is; they hate my guts. Good for her if she moved. Seems like we both said to each other every year that we couldn't stay here for another, no way. But if she's still around—I mean, it's only been five years. Stranger shit has come to pass than a couple of lovers getting back together, right? There's always a chance.

I wouldn't say I've been looking for her, exactly, but I've come down here by myself and had drinks different nights in all the places we used to go to. I couldn't blame her for not coming down here anymore. It's gotten a lot dingier, even looks dangerous in some spots. Besides, it starts to make your whole chest hurt when you can't look at a booth in a bar without thinking about one of the best times of your life that happened there and how now it's gone forever. You feel yourself disappearing.

Flashing lights come on behind us. Shit. I've got to think. He lets the siren whoop once. Does he just want to get by? No, he's pulling off to the shoulder right behind us and slowing down at the exact same pace, like our cars are connected by a rope. I should have known. After dark, in a neighborhood like this, cop sees an older car with a bunch of heads bobbing around in it, he thinks: Kids out partying. They used to pull us over for no reason at all. When I had long hair, they'd frisk us and search the car. That's how they get their jollies, these bastards.

"Are we stopping?" Winona asks, as I gradually bring us to a halt. There's a definite note of alarm in her voice. "Where are we?" she demands. This isn't going to be pretty.

"My business has taken me to ports of call in countries all over the world," Norm assures us.

"Is it lightning?" asks Heidi. She means the cop car's lights flashing through the windows from behind us. "An electrical malfeasance. The power comes and goes away."

"License and registration," the cop says, shining his flashlight in my face. The authoritative voice shuts everybody else up. I used to wonder why cops prefer those flashlights with the long heavy handles till I got bashed over the head with one. That made it pretty clear. I get out my license and hand it to the cop. Then I lean over to open the glove compartment.

"Washington State," the cop says, like he's not sure if it's a real U.S. state. "This license is from Washington State."

"How 'bout them apples?" Norm says, and then laughs heartily.

The cop shines his light in the back seat and Winona screams bloody murder. The cop sort of hops backwards.

Now what? It seems somebody stuffed the glove box full of feathers. I pull some out, hold them up to the light and remember. I toss them back in. A few of the pieces flutter down onto Beatrice's lap.

By now the car has erupted with conflicting realities. Winona is shrieking, "I'm an American citizen!" over and over. "I'm an American citizen of the United States!"

"What does it want?" Heidi asks. Then sounds like she's reciting poetry as she says, "If and then from spaceship young hooligans of evening come."

"We miss our flight," Norm says, "and then we miss our connecting flight, and the conference, and it's déjà vu all over again."

Beatrice starts to hum that tune about England's green and pleasant land, apparently to keep herself calm. Even in the dim light, I can see her face has the same tension in it as when Maylene comes over. Her hands are folded in her lap and I give them a quick pat.

The cop bends down and sticks his head right in the car, looking past me into the back seat. I imagine rolling up the window on his neck. He shines his light around. Winona starts screaming again, and Heidi starts screaming in response, and Norm raises his voice and tries to talk over them. The cop steps back, the look on his face is like somebody who just found he's sunk hip-deep in shit.

"Officer," I say, over the racket, "we're on our way to an Alzheimer's meeting at Deaconess Hospital."

"Oh," he says, handing my license back. He didn't get a chance to find the expiration date, thank God. He straightens up all the sudden. "Ma'am," he says, with a tone of reprimand. He calls over the roof of the car again, "Ma'am."

I look over and see the passenger door is standing open. Beatrice is gone. The cop calls to her again, and starts going after her. But she's already opening the passenger door of his cruiser.

"Stay here," I tell the others. When I get over to the cop car, he's trying to coax the radio transmitter out of Beatrice's hand. A scratchy voice that sounds like it's trapped under water and is concerned to know what in the hell is going on, comes out of the speaker. The cop yanks the transmitter out of Beatrice's hand right quick and lets it know everything's okay. As I start shepherding Beatrice back to her car, the cop pops out for a second to tell me to be sure and get that left tail light fixed.

In the car, Norm is entertaining the ladies with a lecture about global trade relations. They're all much calmer, but Winona has both arms wrapped around her hat box like one of us might try to tear it away from her.

The woman at the front desk of the hospital says she doesn't know anything about any Alzheimer's music recital. But she calls someone who does, and we get on the elevator to go to the room where the others are already waiting for us.

"Are we sick?" Winona keeps asking on the elevator. "Have we become ill?"

Norm stands watching the floor numbers change over the door with his hands clasped behind his back. "This is no way to run a business," he muses. "Not at all."

We find the room. It has a low plywood stage with a piano on it at one end. A bunch of folding chairs are set up facing it. There are folding tables disguised with paper tablecloths lining one wall, soft drinks and snacks on them. I see a few of the people from daycare, but most are from the dementia ward here. Some are dressed regular and some are in hospital gowns. A couple of them are in wheelchairs. They all have nametag stickers on them.

Beverly comes hurrying over, her stockings making that arousing whisking sound between her thighs. This is an event: she's dressed up, with a blouse that has this big floppy bow that hangs down from the neck. She even got her hair cut; it's still the strawberry blond, feathered-back do, just abbreviated.

"Thank goodness you made it," she says to me. She's a little paler than usual, she's so nervous. Also, she got taller.

A small man, whose head looks like a skull with a thin layer of skin stretched over it, wanders up and stands by us like he's waiting to be introduced. His nametag says "Elmer."

"Well, we hit a little bump along the way, I guess you could say," I tell Beverly.

Her face drops. She gets even paler, so you can see the tiny freckles that usually are hardly noticeable, across her delicate nose and full cheeks. "You weren't in an accident, were you?"

"Oh, no. Nothing to worry about," I say. "Your hair looks good," I add, and that brings a little color back to her face as she glances down. But before she can say anything, a businessy looking woman comes over and tells Bev she'd like to get things started. Beverly introduces me to her, some hospital administrator.

"I'm Elmer," says Elmer, and makes a little bow to each of us in turn.

When Beverly turns around, I see she's only taller because she's wearing high heels. I also see her big calves—she's wearing those stockings that have a seam going up the back. Jesus Christ almighty! Does she do these things just to see if she can drive me completely insane? You'd think she didn't have any idea that those seams are like little highways for the imagination, leading right up under the pleats of her dress. You might even believe she's totally oblivious to how every step she takes in those heels makes her ass bulge out from one side to the other in a kind of rolling wave of buttocks. Not me. It's a scandal is what it is. God damn it. And just for that, I'd like to hustle her off to an examining room somewhere and play a real rough game of doctor.

It takes a little while to get our people sorted out from the hospital people and all rounded up on the stage. I sit in the audience, in the back row with Joanne and Cliff on either side of me. And now, watching the stage as Beverly hits the first notes of "You Are My Sunshine," it strikes me how weird this might look to an outsider. Seeing these people in daycare all the time like I do, you don't notice. But with them on a stage and an audience focused on them, every quirk seems magnified. I mean, for starters, they're almost all way off key. Some are even singing words to other songs. Phil, who's sort of leaning against Beatrice, doesn't sing at all. Just stands there, shaking some, with his mouth hanging open. Winona has her suitcase standing beside her, and she's still holding the hatbox. Norm stands ramrod straight and beats his cowbell a little harder than usual. Virginia, the theater woman, is wearing some ancient blue ball gown with more glitter on it than her usual getups have. And she's got a matching feather boa for the occasion. Midway through the third song, she starts swaying around, waving the boa from the ends of each arm, now and then smacking somebody else in the face with it. The tambourine appears in the air and quivers just over Phil's head, attached to a frail forearm. Deidre's in the house. Didn't know she was even here tonight.

But the audience is just as bad. Some of them get up and walk around. Some look at the walls instead of the stage, and others talk to each other like this is just the opening act for what they really came to see.

I glance to my left at Cliff, who's sitting real straight with his hands on his knees, his chin held high, the way people do at patriotic events. He's a little apprehensive and you can see why—his wife is near the edge of the stage and keeps kind of tottering around in an unsteady little circle. On the other side of me, Joanne is holding her rosary in her lap, murmuring something with her eyes half closed. I try to imagine the look that might appear on her face if someone biffed the back of her head and said, "Wake up!"

After a while, an elderly woman in a hospital gown stands up in the second row and claps along with the music, with her hands over her head, swaying from side to side, like she's at a Grateful Dead show.

Harvey decides to go for a walk, dinging his triangle as he goes by the piano, where Beverly, who looks like she might be sick, misses a note but keeps on playing. Harvey steps down from the stage and strikes his triangle.

"Good lord," says Cliff.

Harvey walks slowly past the front of the stage, real solemn, dinging the triangle every other step. A few people begin to clap as he drifts by the front of the room and right on out the door. The song comes to an end—not all at once, because some folks are singing a few words, or a line or two, behind—then from out in the hall comes a single, "Ding!"

Cliff is out of his seat and heading for the door. I'm slow on the uptake because while it's happening, it seems to me like Harvey's performing a magic trick. The way he glided out while everyone else was singing, his triangle held in front of him like Diogenes' lamp, he looked free. Like he found a way to use a musical instrument to extract himself from his time and place in the world.

By the time I rouse myself to go help Cliff, he and the administrator lady are guiding Harvey by his elbows back into the room, where he's greeted by a scattered ovation. The collapsed side of his face doesn't register this and neither does the normal side as he's helped back to his place on the platform.

So what the fuck is the matter with me? Harvey hasn't achieved nirvana—he's lost, a victim of a terrible disease that's eating his mind. I have to wake the hell up! Someone should smack me upside the head.

When the recital is over, I find myself standing with a paper cup of pop by the goodies table with Beverly, who's pretty well traumatized, and the administrator lady who put name stickers on everybody except herself. She says, "I think it's gone pretty well, considering."

Considering what, I wonder—that there could have been a fire? Or that she was expecting there to be casualties?

"Yes," Beverly says, through the blank sheet of paper her face has turned into. "We have done better in practices, I have to say. But it really did go fine, really." The poor thing is trying so hard to convince herself. Come here, let me take you in my arms, you big succulent goose.

"I'm so glad we finally got the opportunity to have you all here," the administrator says. But she's scanning the room even now for potential disasters. Not inspired. Nope. I don't reckon she'll be starting an inpatient choir any time soon.

I don't know if mingle is the right word for what I start to do here, but I somehow end up talking to several people. A shrill woman with a walker, whose nametag says "Vera," tells me she's trying to find her eight -year-old son. She hasn't seen him since this morning and she's teetering on the edge of a serious panic attack. So never mind it's not physically possible for her to have a son this age. I ask her to describe what he looks like. We go around the room looking under folding food tables and chairs till she forgets what we're looking for.

What's more disconcerting than Elmer's skull with eyeballs and big bat ears, is the fact that he's the liveliest person here. "I do a little soft-shoe, you know," he tells me.

"Really," I say.

"Yeah, yeah, yeah, sure," he says. "Been all over the world, all over. Here watch." Then he starts saying, "Dot, dot, dot, da, da—cha! Dot, dot, da, da, da—cha!" looking down at the linoleum and stamping all around like he's trying to kill bugs or something. When he moves his legs you can see by how they press against his pants that they're about the size of my arms, which are pretty skinny. He lifts his own scrawny arms over his head, snaps his fingers, twirls around and almost pitches himself face-first into a basket of potato chips on one of the tables. He's panting, and a little bit embarrassed when I reach out to steady him. "You get the idea," he says.

One woman here wants me to understand she's only in this place because she just gave birth to another toaster. A man asks me if I'll go over his portfolio with him before the end of the week. Certainly. Beatrice seems to strike up a friendship with a woman who talks about gardenias while Beatrice talks about planting corn. She keeps Phil's sleeve clutched tight in one fist.

Basically, this has the feel of a 60th high school reunion where everybody's peaking on some real good acid. And there are some downers. I try to avoid Cliff when I sense him watching me from the other side of the room. Maybe he wants to commiserate, or tell me about his support group again. I don't know. Whenever I talk to him, I feel like I'm being found out. I'm a fraud, it's true. I miss the old Beatrice. In spite of what I say, of course I'd rather have her coherent again. But she's not nearly as bad as Mildred. And unlike Cliff, I'm not seeing her through the lens of a forty-seven year marriage. If Carla had this disease, I'd need more than a support group. Probably I'd just go berserk and maybe kill myself. Cliff has to share his pain because it's too much for one person. Maybe he even hates my guts because mine isn't.

I see Joanne opening a big Tupperware and arranging more cupcakes on a platter that didn't have too many missing. The sight of her doing this depresses the hell out of me. All told, there must be a hundred cupcakes for crying out loud. With crappy canned icing. I can't help picturing Joanne at home with some old gospel record playing on the hi-fi, dutifully stirring, pouring and filling the accordion paper cups half-full of box-mix glop for Jesus. Then after they're baked, going along real satisfied, filling the plastic boxes with cupcakes because that's what gets God happy. This is her life. Why do you have to knock it? If she enjoys doing this, what's the matter it? Nothing. Only the fact she enjoys it is awful.

6

The amigos have landed. When I get to work on Monday morning the pit is already full of them, jabbering away in Spanish. Wade is long gone. We legals are outnumbered by far. The language barrier is keeping Terry from dumping all the debris off his truck. You raise the bed, then stomp hard on the gas so when the truck jerks forward all the branches and shit slide off. But usually some of the stuff gets hung up on the sides, so you back up and do it again. What you need is somebody standing back there so you can just glance in your mirror, and they let you know when it's all off or to step on it again.

Terry knows a few Spanish words. He keeps yelling at the Mexican guy he can see in his mirror, "Finito? Finito?" There's a lot of noise because someone is also driving the Bobcat around the pit.

"Tienes que ir una vez más," the guy says.

"What?" yells Terry.

I'm about to help out, but Ryan comes into the pit just then and stands in front of me going through a file folder. "As I alluded to before, John, now that the amigos are here, you'll be taking a truck out."

Over his shoulder, I see one of the Mexicans, a wiry little guy, climb up the steep hill of Terry's raised truck bed to pull loose the tree branch that's holding up a bunch of debris. The guy behind Terry's truck is holding a finger up, saying, "Espera, espera," a word Terry obviously doesn't know because he guns the engine and the truck jumps forward.

I yell, but it's too late. The guy on the truck bed does a backward somersault and lands on his back in the pile of leaves and branches that come off the truck with him. There's a burst of Spanish cuss words and we all go rushing over to where a couple guys are pulling the little one to his feet. None of them are what you'd call big, or even average in U.S. size, but this one who took the fall is specially tiny. His dark eyes are peeled wide. Amazingly, he's not hurt. He has a broad face and a small thin nose under which he's wearing this big black handlebar mustache that looks like a ridiculous disguise. Or maybe the opposite of a disguise. I mean, it makes it too easy to picture him wearing a big old poncho and sombrero, selling tacos. He walks around a little bit and before long another jolly looking guy with a round belly is calling him pendejo and laughing. The little guy shoves him and tells him to shut up.

These two are the ones I'll be working with, Ryan tells me. Carlos is the one who took a dive, the other is Filipe. Ryan gives me the contract for the job and the list of materials I need. There are four crews, now that the amigos are here, and mine is the runt. We have the shittiest truck and the shittiest tools. Then when we get to the job and there are all kinds of other trucks, plumbers and masons parked all over the place, I realize I can add to that list. We got the shittiest job too.

"Well now the party can really start," says this enormous plumber with a tool belt, when I walk into the back yard. There's a crater in the ground that's being turned into a swimming pool with a waterfall and other man-made rock formations all around it. The whole yard is a mud pit with trucks parked every which way.

"They're on vacation," the plumber tells me, talking about the owners. "Supposably they want to come home to a whole new yard. That's why they scheduled us all at the same time."

Carlos and Filipe are still out front unloading our tools. Another truck is going to be coming soon from the tree farm and there's no way he could get back here even if I got everybody else to move their trucks. When I look at our list of plants, I see we have big stuff coming. Some of them are going to have burlap-wrapped root balls that weigh three hundred pounds. It's going to take most of the day just getting our plants back here. And we have no Bobcat. We have a tree cart and wheelbarrows.

I'm looking over the blueprints Ryan gave me so I'll know where to put all the stupid shit. The plumber comes over to me. "Hey, do you know anything about real estate?" he asks.

"Not much," I say.

He grabs at his crotch and says, "Would you call this a lot? Ha, ha, ha!"

I can see this is going to be one long-ass week. It's a challenge to even walk around back here. The mud glues itself to the bottom of your boots. So when you're not sliding and falling down, and you actually manage to lift your foot to step forward, you find your boots now weigh about twenty pounds each and the soles are so lumpy that you wobble around like you're on stilts.

At one point, as Carlos is going by him with a wheelbarrow full of smaller plants, the happy-go-lucky plumber stops him to try his joke on him. After he tells him the opening line, Carlos says, "Lo siento, pero no hablo Inglés."

"No, no," says the plumber, raising his voice, like speaking a different language means deafness. "I'm saying, do you know anything about real estate?"

Carlos shrugs. The plumber delivers his punch line and laughs at it again. Carlos smiles politely and in Spanish basically tells the plumber he's a great big stupid asshole gringo. My high-school Spanish sucks, but I learned a lot more of the important stuff standing on a line cleaning fish than they teach you in a classroom.

At lunch, Carlos and Filipe break out the beans, rice and tortillas. Filipe leans on his elbow in the grass in a corner of the yard and points out how if somebody in Mexico had all the land these people have, they'd grow food on it. Not pay to decorate it with plants you can't even eat. He can't understand it. I try to explain in my pidgin Spanish that we are a wealthy but backward people. That a visual impression of affluence is supposed to make up for an impoverished lifestyle—bland food, empty entertainment. Our conversation reminds me of how Carla told me once that some tribes of Native Americans didn't even understand the concept of private ownership of land. So that made it a whole lot easier for the Europeans to take it off them.

The cultural exchange with Carlos and Filipe helps the time go by faster, I hate to say. I always swore I'd never be one of those working stiffs who just wants the day to be over. Because that just means, in daily installments, you're wanting your life to be over. Which means your life isn't anything more than a failure to commit suicide. But, well, here I am.

We get half the plants in the ground by noon on Wednesday. In spite of the chaos of this place. If Ryan's going to come by the job it's usually when he figures you'll be eating lunch. That way, he can discuss the job with you without paying you because he doesn't pay for you to eat lunch, just like he doesn't pay you to ride in the truck. So we go slopping around the muddy yard together and he decides he doesn't like where most of the plants are and goes sticking his little flags in the ground where he wants them moved to. It's kind of demoralizing to dig up a tree you just planted to move it over a couple feet and replant it. But that's what Carlos, Filipe and I are going to spend the rest of today and part of tomorrow doing, looks like. I grumble that Ryan could have stopped by earlier in the week.

He stops walking. We're at the back fence line. He looks at me, scrunching his face in the sun, his foreheaded brain squirming beneath the brim of his new hair. "Don't you like this job, John?" he asks.

I'm not sure he means this particular location, or Rinky Dink landscaping in general. "I followed those plans you gave me," I say, my voice not exactly concealing the fact that I'm a little pissed. I stick my hand out at the blue spruce trees that are staggered along the fence line. It's a retarded landscaping idea in the first place. "The spacing is exactly what the plans said it should be."

"I realize that," Ryan says. "And I realize that from your perception, what I'm asking you to do might seem to be like a Sophoclean task. But I gotta think about the big picture, see? The way I look at it, you're batting, right? But I'm the coach. I can see the whole field from where I'm at. You see? So there's the issue called aestheticism I gotta take care of from over here on the sidelines. That's the way it is. You sometimes might be too wrapped-up in the game to see everything I can see."

He gets this squinting-from-the-dugout expression on his face, which you can tell he thinks is the look of a visionary, as he gazes down the property line to where the masons are building their bogus waterfall by the pool. Carlos and Filipe have finished their burritos and are sitting in the shade on one of the few un-muddy patches of lawn in the corner. They take sideways glances at us, not sure if they should get back to work or what.

Ryan raises his heavy gold watch. "Would you look at that. I gotta get over to Terry's job, then I got an appointment with a contractor." He slaps my shoulder. "All right buddy?" he says.

With a few disgusting slurping noises, we both manage to get our feet out of the mud we've been sinking into. Then we can walk again. Ryan gives a thumbs-up to Carlos and Filipe from across the yard and yells, "Caliente! Caliente!" Then he gets in his truck and drives off. I don't know what the hell he thinks he's saying, but we don't need anybody to tell us it's warm. We've been sweating all morning.

Summer oozes into the Nasty like airborne gravy. Sometimes the humidity is so thick it looks like fog and it hangs around for weeks, pasting your clothes to you and making it hard to breathe. You get so used to your skin being sticky that when you first get out of the shower you feel like somebody peeled your skin off. But in about three minutes all your pores are little bitty puddles again and you sink back into your amphibian stupor. I don't like how summertime in this country is marketed just like New Year's Eve. You're supposed to be having the time of your life with a bunch of super-great friends but really you just hang around feeling uncomfortable, wishing it was over.

One night, Maylene calls me to ask if I forgot I'm taking Beatrice to the doctor tomorrow. No, I say, I've got the appointment marked right there on the calendar on the kitchen wall. I can't wait.

But Doctor Cornelius Lipscomb can. Even though we're on time, he means to make us wait in the waiting room with the TV broadcasting women who remind me of Maylene and discuss skin products that they promise will make Beatrice and me look ten years younger. They're all excited like they're informing us of the invention of an actual time-travel machine they just took a ride on. A young mother here with us watches patiently while her son throws magazines across the room. I have to admit, I like being here in the air conditioning better than being out there in the heat I can see waving off the asphalt outside, which is where I could be, sweating over getting a sapling in the ground or whatever other dumb thing Ryan had in mind for me today.

A physician's assistant comes into the waiting room and takes us to a little white room where she takes Beatrice's blood pressure and temperature and tells us Dr. Lipscomb will be right there and leaves us alone again.

"What time is it?" Beatrice asks.

I make up a time. We wait. Beatrice gets up off the examining table and starts opening drawers and cupboards. She takes out a handful of tongue depressors, puts some on the counter and some in her pockets. She gets out several pairs of surgical gloves and masks. I'm not about to stop her. If the good doctor would deign to keep his schedule, this wouldn't be happening.

"Whoah!" Beatrice says. "My goodness gracious!" Something falls from her hands, she wobbles and takes a couple steps backward. I jump up to steady her, then get her to sit down on a swivel stool by the counter. Her eyes are real wide. As she sits down, I notice Beatrice's hair, secure in its bun, is a little greasy looking. It smells kind of like garbage.

I pick up a little white packet off the floor. When I bring it close enough to my face to read the tiny lettering, it's like a claw going up my nose the way it clears my sinuses. Smelling salts. Beatrice broke this one open. She's sitting there quietly now, pulling on a pair of latex gloves.

Dr. Lipscomb comes in, introduces himself and shakes my hand. Beatrice gets up and shakes his hand with one of hers that's prepared for surgery. He smiles at her and the little mess she's made on the counter with that superior, detached attitude they teach these fuckers in medical school.

"So, how can we help you?" Beatrice asks.

"Well, first by just answering a few questions," he says, glancing down at his clipboard, then putting it on the counter. "Beatrice," he announces. "Can you tell me what day of the week it is?"

She says she certainly can. He waits a second but she doesn't offer. So he rephrases. "It's Thursday," she says. She's off by a couple of days, but what would you expect? Her days are mostly the same. She doesn't need to know their names.

"What month are we in?" Dr. Lipscomb asks. He's smiling like he's happy to get back at her for making him ask her twice about the day of the week.

Beatrice looks at me, but I stay quiet. Her eyes dart around the room for clues. "It's January," she says, but it's June. Close enough—they both start with J.

"And what is the date?" the doctor asks, softly. "Including the year."

Beatrice rubs at her little Pixie nose with a latex thumb. "Well, smarty pants, why don't you tell me?" she says. "You're supposed to be the fireman."

Dr. Lipscomb picks up his clipboard and starts jotting something. "Count backward from twenty for me, will you?"

"Twenty, nineteen, tenteen, eleven… oh, heck. Why do you want to know these things?" Beatrice demands. She's pretty angry by now, quivering the way she does when Maylene's around. She keeps balling her blouse up in her fist like she's getting ready to tear it off. "What time is it anyway?" she asks Dr. Lipscomb.

But he's scribbling away on his clipboard again. "I'm going to give you a prescription to fill for her," he says to me, like Beatrice just walked out of the room even though she's right in front of him.

"What for?" I ask.

"Something that will help," he says. "And moderate her moods."

"She needs choline therapy," I say. That gets him to stop writing. "This whole problem is caused by aluminum. You know that as well as I do. It's keeping her neurotransmitters from working."

"Now, there's no real proof of that," Dr. Lipscomb says, putting the clipboard back down and folding his arms.

I can't stand these arrogant bastards. I decide to just unload on this one. "Did you know that fluoride is a waste product from when they manufacture aluminum?" I say.

"Well—"

"And you know who started the policy of putting it in our drinking water? A public health official who'd been a lawyer for the aluminum industry, that's who."

With his one arm still across his chest, Dr. Lipscomb raises the other, puts his index finger under his nose, furrows his brow and looks at me like my breath is stinking up the place.

"And the fluoride," I go on, "that shit makes your body absorb the aluminum even faster." I don't know about this part—I just made it up on the spot, but it sounds convincing, the way I say it. "So what the hell are you prescribing, Valium?"

"I was going to try haloperidol first, but then Valium—"

"Wait, isn't that the one that causes side effects that makes it look like you've got Parkinson's? All this shit you wanna give her only hides the problem. And I'm not gonna give it to her. You're not going to turn her into a zombie you fucking asshole."

"I'll be back in a moment," he says, and leaves. Beatrice smiles at me from the stool she's gone back to. She swivels back and forth slow and hums one of the songs they sang at the recital.

"So why doesn't the AMA come out with warnings about aluminum, Cornelius?" I ask him when he comes back. "I'll tell you why—it's because all you fucks are getting paid off by the drug companies that make the shit like what you're trying to shove down Beatrice's throat."

A security guard the size of a decent tool shed comes in the door Dr. Lipscomb left open. He asks me to come with him. His hands are so big the thumb and middle finger overlap as he grabs hold of my upper arm and walks me past the nurse station.

"What?" I keep saying. "What'd I do?" He takes me down the stairs even though the elevator seems to be working fine. Then it's out the door and into the blazing parking lot where he finally lays off my arm and with me still asking what.

"You know what," he says. "Now you can shut the fuck up and wait out here until the doctor is through. I'll be right inside." He points with one of the bratwursts his hands are made out of at the waiting room on the other side of the glass. "I'll be keeping an eye on you." And there he stands, leaning against the desk, chatting in the air conditioning with the reception lady, looking over at me now and then. I pace around, smoke cigarettes and try to look like I don't give a shit, till Beatrice comes out.

That night I write PILLKILL on a billboard that advertises health insurance. They haven't changed any of the ads yet on the billboards I painted before. What you have to do is get them right after the new ad is up because they already paid for however many months to have that space. On an ad for a computer, I write SCREENSLAVERS. SCREAMFLAVORS is what Gary writes on the next one after that.

"Dude, are you mocking me?" I ask, as we're driving by our new work. Gary's already got a joint going.

"Now why would I go and do that?" he asks, and passes me the joint. What the hell. I take it. I've been pissed off all day and all night.

"You know," I say, "I'm not sure you get it."

"Oh," he says, nodding. He lifts a hand from the steering wheel and scratches at the side of his bushy head. "Yeah, probably you're right. I don't get it. What you do is so deep, man."

All the sudden I see he's got a good point. I'm the dumb-ass. A preachy graffiti artist. How big of a hypocrite can you be? Besides, words are just other weapons they use. I mean, you put a spike in one lousy tree and it's "eco-terrorism." But you clear-cut thousands of acres of trees and somehow it's not.

I don't know why, except that I'm feeling disgusted with myself, but I write PLACENTACAKES on the next billboard. Gary does two more: SAVE BABY SEMEN on an anti-abortion billboard, and LOVEBUGS ME on a billboard advertising a store.

After work the next day, I come home and Beatrice is sitting there flipping through a magazine. Without any pants on; her shriveled Pixie legs crossed at the knee. "How was school, dear?" she asks.

"All right," I say. "What happened to your pants?"

She looks down at her thighs, the loose skin, purple veins, like they might belong to someone else. "It got too hot," she says.

I'm going to let this slide, I'm so tired from work and from last night. All I want is to get out of my own stiff, mud-caked pants and take a shower. But I remember Beatrice's hair. I convince her to let me wash it in the kitchen sink. It's a good thing there's this big tub of a wash basin in here. Makes things easier. I undo the bun and Beatrice's long, thinning gray hair falls down almost to her elbows in greasy clumps.

"Is it nice?" she asks, stroking it like it's a cat on her shoulder.

"Yes," I say. "You're as pretty as ever."

The fact of the matter is she looks crazy, like somebody who's come completely unraveled. She doesn't have to bend too far over the sink, she's so little. I run water over her head.

"Oh, frosty, frosty!" she says, so I add more hot.

As I'm lathering up her hair I notice brownish gray patches behind her ears and on the back of her neck. Is this some weird part of the aging process? Your skin starts to get like rotting fruit? Oh shit—no. Looking closer I can see it's dirt.

"That was nice," Beatrice says, as I towel her hair dry.

Her cheeks are rosier from leaning over. I can't help it, I plant a kiss on one. I tell her it's time for a bath and I take her upstairs, turn the water on for her like always, then leave. But this time I peek in a few minutes later and see she's not taking a bath at all. She's sitting on the closed toilet lid reading a steam-rumpled paperback she got off a shelf nearby.

I guess I heard all those horror stories from Cliff and other folks at daycare. But Beatrice doesn't get paranoid too often. She hasn't ever accused me of trying to poison her or steal her things. A couple times we had arguments about what she's going to wear and whether or not I've been hiding the sugar. Which I do sometimes because once she ate a whole bowl of it and threw up.

But this is my first real fight with Beatrice. She screams at me. She's scared to death of the water. I'm on the verge of just picking her up and plopping her in there like a lobster. Finally, she lowers herself in, clinging to me, crying, her wrinkled, saggy body shaking uncontrollably. I remember bathing my dog when I was a kid and how he fought me. When he got wet you could see all his bones through the hair and he shivered and looked at me with his eyes big and mournful just like this.

Beatrice has forgotten what to do. I have to demonstrate, even hold her one hand with the soap in it and her other with the washcloth and rub them together. I end up mostly having to wash her myself. I can't bring myself to do her chest, with those breasts hanging there like withered balloons. I coax her into doing it. It's terrible enough having to run the washcloth over her hunched back. Her spine sticks out like a row of knobs just under the skin.

When it's over and I get her dressed and settled down again, I go to my room and close the door. I sit on the bed looking at the trees all around me, which Beatrice painted for me. The Pixies climbing the walls, the stars on the dark ceiling. And I cry. For a while. It's a relief. Kind of like barfing from the heart.

Next week Filipe is gone, along with most of the other Mexicans who were working with us. They've been replaced by a new batch. Carlos is still with me and we have this new guy, Alejandro, who's missing half his teeth and smells like stale refried beans and cervezas. In the truck, he picks his nose for a few minutes and then nods off to sleep with his head on Carlos's shoulder. I ask Carlos what happened to everybody else. My Spanish is so bad he has to explain more than once that they didn't get paid two weeks in a row. Then he makes a motion with his hands, one glancing off the other fast and shooting ahead, which means that the other guys took off.

As the season wears on, I start to feel like I'm digging my way through a bottomless summer. I sweat till my shirt is soaked, take it off and work till my shoulders burn, put another shirt on, soak through that, repeat. Planting boxwoods, hydrangea, thread leaf maples, weeping cherries, euonymus and pachysandra. A jumble of job sites in Clifton, Hyde Park, Mt. Carmel, Madeira, Montgomery and Blue Ash.

The Nasty was named after Cincinnatus, a Roman general who put down his war hatchet and picked up a plow. Which, when you really look at it, is kind of a joke because this isn't a place to do any serious farming. You stick a shovel in the ground anyplace within a hundred miles of the Nasty, you're going to come up with clay. Cincinnatus would have done better to pick up a potter's wheel. I mean if he were to bury the hatchet here.

But this area is full of all kinds of outside jokes like that. On the East side, in Hyde Park, people go around with their noses in the air like they're in Hyde Park, because most of them don't know there's a real one in London. And if anyone came here from Germany and saw this ghetto version of Over-the-Rhine, I bet they'd think we were making fun of them. We're not. We just don't know no better because we never been nowhere. There ain't no reason to travel—we got Paris, Kentucky right nearby! And Florence too. So shut up! Just be happy about it. Buy a fucking donut. Whatever. You might as well get comfortable. Sit back, relax, turn on the TV, put your feet up, and die.

Sometimes, while I'm digging, I wonder what happened when Carla went on her dig in Mexico. Because it wasn't too long after that she started to change. When I met her, she was still finishing her degree. Not because she was stoned, like Gary, but because she was double majoring in anthropology and archeology and working her way through.

Needless to say, she didn't work at the bookstore for very long after she told-off our manager at that meeting. I could never have gone back into a place I got fired from and risk the embarrassment of seeing the people who fired me, but it didn't seem to bother Carla. One day she came in and put a few magazines and an expensive hardcover book about lost civilizations on the counter by my register.

"I want to return these," she said. "And with the store credit you give me, I'd like to buy them back again." She made an exaggerated wink.

I knew I had to ask her out—now or never. As I was putting the stuff in a bag for her, I said, "Did you find everything okay?"

"You know," she said, "after you die that's exactly the question God asks you. But it's up to you to make sure the answer is going to be yes."

Carla's eyes are dark brown, almost as dark as the pupils. It seemed like this was what always made it hard to tell what she was thinking. Especially about me.

"Well, may I have my purchases?" she asked.

I was still holding the bag, and not out to her. "Yeah. If I can still take you up on that shot. But after my shift." Hard to believe what a dork I was then.

"Deal," she said.

That night we were at a bar and a guy came up and sat on a stool on the other side of her and offered to buy her a drink. Maybe he didn't notice me next to her, or more likely, didn't care. He was dressed like a professional and was several years older than us.

Carla put down the pint she was drinking. "So you want to buy me a beer and you're thinking maybe later we can fuck," she said.

"Well..." the guy chuckled and looked at her with a hopeful smile meant to show his roguish charm. I stood up and was trying to put together the words of some cooler and maybe more menacing version of, "Hey pal, why don't you buzz off and leave the lady alone."

But then Carla said, real loud, "You want to fuck me?"

The guy flinched. Conversations stopped all around us. He looked around and said, "Hey, um—"

"You want to fuck me!" Carla yelled. "I can't believe it! You're saying you want to fuck me!"

The bartender was on his way over, but already the guy in the suit was off his stool, backing away, shaking his hands around in front of him like to clean off a window, going, "No, no, sorry, Jesus, no." Everybody was looking at him like he just tried to rape Carla, and he high-tailed it right out the door.

Carla turned back to the bar and took a swig of beer. "What a jackass," she said.

It scared the hell out of me. Because there I was. And, I mean, I did want to fuck her. But even if she'd wanted to go somewhere with me right that minute I wouldn't have been able to. How she demolished that guy made my dick shrivel up like a dead worm.

But it came back to life a few weeks later when we had sex for the first time. And eventually we moved in together. I thought it was all settled after that; we were going to be like everybody else, just way different. Carla got a job at the University, and was trying to pay down her debts before she applied to graduate school. I was job-hopping, like I've always done ever since.

The advantage of not having a career is, any time you want, you can say fuck this and walk off your job. And the minute you do, you're powerful, you get a soaring sense of freedom, you can do anything, the possibilities are endless. At least for a couple weeks. Then you're feverishly grabbing butts out of the ashtray to smoke what's left of them, counting through the change jar, saying Oh shit oh shit oh shit, what in the fuck am I gonna do?

I couldn't see the point of college and so didn't stick with it. Carla finished and then spent three months digging in Mayan ruins in Mexico when we were both about twenty-two. One of her professors told her about this scholarship and she got to go for free. I spent most of that three months moping around our apartment, waiting for her occasional phone call.

When she came back, with brown Myan skin and pictures of the site with her and the other archeologists, there was something wrong. She wasn't excited to tell me about it. She looked over the pictures with me like she was looking at some stranger's family vacation photos. We started going out with the usual crowd again, but while everyone else was drinking and laughing, Carla stayed distant. Sometimes even now I feel like I'm still waiting for her to come back from Mexico. It made everybody uncomfortable because she'd always been the one telling stories or goofing on somebody. Now she just sat there, bored.

I was relieved when she said she was going to start graduate school soon. We were sitting in our living room—well, our only room besides the bedroom, which fit a bed and not much else—and Carla was slouched on the couch, endlessly clicking through the channels. Something she'd started to do a lot. Like she was trying to find a new channel.

I didn't think I'd heard right, for starters. Because it sounded like she said she wanted to get an MBA. I said, "You can't get into the NBA, you're a girl." She didn't bother to roll her eyes or anything. She was slouched so far she was almost lying down, her chin resting on her collar bone. She pressed the remote control like she was firing a gun.

"There isn't any money in artifacts," she said. "I can tell you that."

"But what about all your studies?" I said.

"Fantasy," she said.

I wished she'd never gone to Mexico. "But you're not interested in business stuff," I said.

Carla clicked off the television and tossed the remote control on the couch. "Look," she said, "you can be interested in a lot of things. You can study a lot of things. But I don't want to spend my life struggling to get degrees and publish papers in obscure journals just so I can teach other people to do the same thing. I don't even—" she shook her head. A silky brown wave of hair came crashing down and hid the side of her face. "And if you think I want to spend my free time studying mating rituals of some impoverished tribe in Nigeria or go get malaria digging around for shards of pottery in some disgusting jungle, well, you've got another think coming."

&

"What up dawg," Freddie says, when I join him and everybody else in the pit on Friday afternoon. Freddie's from the neighborhood, the only one of us who can walk to work. I'm surprised Ryan hired him. He must have taken some night class on discrimination. Or else listened to cassette tapes about it. Now that I have my own crew, these Friday beer fests are the only time I get to hang out with the other U.S. citizens I work with.

"Damn, John boy—you be sweatin' like muh," Freddie says, and hands me a beer. I say, Speak for yourself, shed my shirt and throw it on the hood of Terry's truck, where it will bake dry in about four minutes. I sit down on the wheel well of the chipper. Years ago, the first time I worked here, I saw a guy get caught in this thing. Turned his hand and forearm into hamburger meat.

Through the open gate of the pit, we can see the Mexicans all piling into their van.

"You know these motherfuckers drive all the way down from Dayton every day?" Terry says.

"And don't even get paid for their work half the time," says Joe, who's pacing around like the caged animal we all are—you feel it for real when you're having your TGIF in a pit full of piles of manure, surrounded by chain link fencing and razor wire.

"Yeah, what's up with that?" I ask.

"Ryan he told me he pays this guy Rodriguez, who's legal, a lump sum for all of 'em," Terry says. He's sitting on the Bobcat trailer, scraping muck from the bottom of his boot with a stick. "It's up to Rodriguez to pay the other guys." He throws his stick into a pile of mulch. "I guess sometimes he don't, so they walk. And so he just rounds up a few more—there sure ain't no shortage of 'em."

"Sheeit," says Freddie. "That is *fuck*ed up."

"Fuck them, dude," Joe says. "My check bounced this week." He waves his hands around while he paces, even though he has a beer in one and a cigarette in the other. No matter how ghetto he acts, his face is always going to make it look like he's about ten years old.

"Ryan's a shyster," I say. "Pure and simple."

Jim-dandy is keeping real quiet. If Ryan told him to turn a blind eye to his shady business practices, Jim would gladly poke his own eyes out. He's having a beer with us—but just one now, then he'll get out of here right quick—only to try and make us believe he wouldn't really stab any of us in the back if he thought it would get him in better with Ryan. He honest-to-God believes landscaping is a career.

I guess it's the way Jim seems to get so much pleasure out of objects, like his little briefcase thingy and the stupid walkie-talkies we have to wear so Ryan can keep tabs on us, that reminds me of Brad. Carla said I was jealous of him and maybe that's true. Maybe I'm jealous of anybody who can walk around so self-assured, who thinks he exists in a perfectly fair, perfectly logical universe because he's got a beeper on his belt or whatever.

Brad seemed to fall into our orbit from a neighboring solar system. He was just there all the sudden. Hanging out with us and our friends. But he wasn't the kind of person Carla and I would normally even talk to. I mean, he was from the East side whereas we both grew up on the West side. He put gel in his hair and drove a brand new sports car. He was going to law school. You could hardly even talk to the prick because he was always making a case for the bass-ackward, materialistic philosophy that shaped his opinions on every single goddamn subject.

Then one time we were at this party and I hadn't seen Carla for a while. I went from the kitchen to the living room and there they were, locked in a passionate embrace. No, no, no. It only seemed that way. What they were locked in was conversation. But her knee was almost touching his. And the way she was turned, leaning toward him, and how she touched his arm—God fucking damn it—she didn't need to be doing that! Why did she have to go and do that? It reminded me of how she paid attention to me, just before our relationship got physical. Which meant she was thinking—Jesus Christ, even now, I can't stand what she was thinking about. And him with that shit-eating grin the whole time.

Just what the hell can you do? My instinct was to go right over there and kick his ass into the middle of next week. But you can't do that, can you? It would only backfire, give Carla the chance to start licking his wounds and speed up the process you couldn't let anyone, specially yourself, see was already underway.

The word cuckold started rolling around in my head. Cuckold, cuckold, cuckold. It's so old-fashioned sounding it has its own kind of dignity to it. Good evening Mr. Cuckold. Your usual table? I trust that the lady is not joining you tonight, is she, Mr. Cuckold? No, of course not. Shall I bring the wine list, Mr. Cuckold, so that you have something to wash down your heart, on which you shall no doubt be dining?

The rest of that night was like there was this other person in my skin. He went around talking to people, laughing extra loud, drinking and smoking, while I stood ripped outside of myself, watching every movement Carla or Brad made. I watched his hands. I gauged the distance their mouths came from each other. It was worse than the worst paranoia you get when you're tripping. Every time Carla's hand moved, I wanted to yell, "Stop! Can't you see he's like a voodoo doll? Every time you touch him it's like you're sinking your fingernails into my bloody heart! Don't laugh at his dumb jokes—don't you see it's a trap!" So I steadily tried to drown myself, one plastic party cup at a time, till I watched me go outside and puke in the bushes.

Jim-dandy's cell phone rings and he talks to his wife. I bet he told her to call him at this exact time so he'd have an excuse to leave early. Terry opens another beer, flicks a beer cap that bounces off his truck.

"I don't get that motherfucker at all," he says, after Jim leaves.

There's a newspaper I'm absently flipping through as the first wave of my buzz starts to relieve the heat and loosen up the soreness of my lower back. Pitch-forking a truckload or two of mulch will play hell on your back. I stop at an article about how this Ohio congressman is trying to get support for a plan to go drilling for oil in the Arctic National Wildlife Refuge. Which I start spluttering out loud about.

"What it always boils down to is there's just too many motherfuckers in the world," Terry says.

"Who cares anyways," says Joe. "We got plenty of land."

"No we don't," I say. Actually, I don't have any idea where this wildlife refuge is. They didn't put one of those mini maps with this article for ignorant people like me. "You ever been to Alaska?" I say. "It's beautiful man. But it's getting fucked up enough with all the cruise ships that're going up there. And now congressman Heighberger here wants to fuck it up completely."

"Heighberger?" says Terry. "We do that motherfucker's landscaping."

When I hear that, I get an idea. Terry goes on to tell me what a royal pain in the ass the guy is. But I pretend to lose interest and let it drop. We talk about other shit for a while. After everybody gets in their cars, half shot in the ass, I go back into the office, burping beer, and flip through the files till I find Heighberger, Thomas and Mary. I write their address on a piece of paper and take it with me.

When the phone rings, I'm reading this novel by Robert Nathan I found on a bookshelf in the dining room. It's full of love and imagination. They don't make novels like this anymore. Or maybe they do. I guess I couldn't really say because I hardly ever read contemporary stuff.

"Dude, we're famous," Gary says.

I ask what he means and he tells me to just turn on the TV. I say I would only there isn't one. I realize now there probably should be, to keep Beatrice company on the days she doesn't go to daycare.

"They're doing a thing on the news about our billboards," Gary says.

Then I hear, "blub, blub, blub, blub," which is the sound, crossing miles of copper wire, of water bubbles as Gary takes a hit from his bong.

"Gary, you okay?" I ask. "Are you calling me from a swimming pool?"

"They're showing one of mine," he says. "Oh, sweet."

Sweet. All the things that are rad in California and wicked in Massachusetts are sweet here. You have to keep this kind of shit straight. Because you can go around the Nasty saying everything under the sun is sweet, but if you told somebody that any one single thing—say, a car—was rad, they'd look at you like you had antennas coming out of your head. And if you walked around Boston saying, "Please?" every time you didn't hear somebody right, well, my guess is they'd come right out and tell you to remove your cranium from your anal cavity and talk like a sensible human being.

"They think ELF is doing it," Gary says.

"Elves?" I say. "They think elves did it?" They're on the evening news blaming shit on elves for Pete's sake. What's the matter with people these days?

"No, ELF," Gary says. "Earth Liberation Front."

"Oh. That's fine. I got no problem with that."

"Oh wow. I am so fucking stoned right now. They're showing that 'Rape Mother' one. I forgot all about that."

"Who was that?" Beatrice asks after I hang up.

"A friend," I say. "Wanted to talk about current events."

"I see," she says.

We usually sit around the living room in the evenings like an old married couple. I read and Beatrice looks through magazines. If I have the energy, I read aloud to her. It doesn't matter if I'm in the middle of a book because she can't follow the story anyway, but it seems to relax her. I really should have thought of getting her a TV before now. I forget what an absent-minded asshole I am until this kind of thing reminds me.

The Heart of It All

The phone rings again. This is definitely some kind of record.

"Oh the bells, bells, bells!" says Beatrice. "What a world of merriment their melody fortells! How they tinkle, tinkle, tinkle, In the icy air of night! While all the stars that oversprinkle All the heavens, seem to twinkle With a crystalline delight."

"That's amazing," I say, letting the phone ring.

"No, that's Poe," says Beatrice. "That's Edgar Stanley Poe."

Sheila's on the phone. She's so sorry she hasn't called sooner. This summer has just been crazy with work and studying for the bar exam and everything. And can I go to a party with her this weekend? Some friends of hers from ski club.

"Ski club?" I say. "Cincinnasty ski club? That's a joke, right—like the Jamaican bobsled team?"

Ow—no. Can tell I gouged her feelings there a little bit. Sheila says she's worried about all the stress I must be having to cope with and she wants me to meet some nice people. So I say okay.

7

At three-thirty a.m. a shattering crash in the kitchen brings me sitting straight up in bed. Burglars. Real clumsy-ass burglars who turned on all the lights downstairs and now are dropping shit all over the floor. Course not. It's another chapter of Beatrice's adventures in the night kitchen. This happens every so often. So I go downstairs, but stop before I turn the corner into the kitchen because I hear her talking. Louder than normal.

"Well, if you'd stay out of the way it wouldn't have happened," she says. As usual, this creeps me out a little, hearing her talk to invisible people. "Now Stanley," she says, "just put that on the counter, sit down, and leave it to me."

Holy shit. Now I'm scared. I force myself to go into the kitchen, half expecting to find my dead grandfather sitting at the table. Instead, I find Beatrice wearing, backwards, the pants and blouse I laid out for her last night. The whole bucket of kitchen utensils that sits on the counter by the stove got scattered all over the floor. There's also a lot of potting soil in little piles all over the place. When she sees me, Beatrice looks cornered. This is what I hate, feeling like Maylene or Stanley, the people who bullied her all her life. She points at the potting soil on the floor, like to lay the blame there.

"This dust," she says, "it went everywhere."

"That was real silly of it," I say. I start getting the spatulas and ladles back in the bucket. I pick up some of the dust. This isn't potting soil, you moron, it's coffee grounds. She was making breakfast.

"I'll get it," I say, when Beatrice stoops down to help. "Just go ahead and do whatever you're doing."

She's relieved; I can see the tension easing out of her bones. She stands up and strokes the top of my head a couple times while I'm wiping the floor. "George," she says. "Always such a sweet boy."

Yeah, sweet as pie. Till he got totally bombed one night and drove his car into a tree, killing himself and my mom. I hadn't been on speaking terms with either of them for years. Which made it easier and harder than I thought.

After I clean the floor, while I'm sitting there waiting for Beatrice to make breakfast, I realize this is all my fault. Beatrice used to get up at night and wander, but lately she's been doing it more, actually starting her day. I've been laying out her clothes the night before, so we wouldn't have to waste time bickering about what she should wear. So now, when she wakes up in the middle of the night, she sees the clothes and thinks it's time to get up and make breakfast.

Beatrice cracks an egg and drops it on the counter next to a bowl. While I'm cleaning this one up, she cracks another and does the exact same thing again. She doesn't like it, but I have to hold her soft, bony hands in my own to guide them so she drops the eggs in the bowl instead of next to it. She uses the whisk okay and manages to make some pieces of French toast. They're not exactly cooked all the way on the one side and the other side is black, but I'm not complaining. When we sit down to eat, Beatrice tries to stick a spoon into her French toast. I have to put the fork and knife in each hand and guide her through a couple practice slices before she gets the hang of it again.

The more coffee I drink, the more sure of it I am every time I say to myself, The fuck if I'm going to work today. Every hour I put in just makes that cocksucker richer. I've got other fish to fry.

"I've got other fish to fry," I say, out loud.

Beatrice smiles at me. Her bun is half undone, strands of gray sticking out and hanging down all around her face. "Always thinking about the next meal before you've even finished the one in front of you, John." Her use of my name is a sign it's probably going to be a good day. "I swear you used to eat faster than I could cook." She reaches across the table and pats the back of my hand.

I call and leave a message for Ryan at the warehouse. As it starts to get light out, I get Beatrice to come into the studio with me. There's a mist hanging over the field, which has gotten taller now with thistle and milkweed and whatnot. A mourning dove is making its lonely who-ing sound from somewhere nearby. Perfect day to start work on my children's book.

One of my favorite Pixies books is *The Pixies Abroad*. One of the Pixies overdoses on old seafaring novels, tells all the rest of them about it, and they get all wound up and go off and steal a square-rigged schooner. Of course, they know as much about sailing as your average Midwesterner. When they climb the ratlines, they climb right over top each other, stepping on the others' heads and hands. They climb out on the yards and fall off the ends of them into the water and have to be thrown life rings and get pulled back on board. Somebody's ankle always gets caught in a line that pulls him right up the mast. A storm almost blows them to pieces. But after a while they get better at it and go sailing off to foreign lands to get into trouble. There are great drawings of Pixies being chased by cannibals in the South Pacific, Pixies dressing up in Chinese robes to go meditate in a Buddhist temple (only because they want to try and levitate), Pixies being chased out of the pyramids by mad mummies they woke up by mistake. The Pixies all put on striped shirts and berets and cough and gag over cigarettes in cafes in Paris. They drink too much beer in an Irish pub and all get sick. And in between, they just go sailing around, playing cards on the deck of their ship, trying to drink rum and spitting it out, giving each other tattoos of anchors on their skinny little arms, petting the whales that surface next to the ship, and making friends with the dolphins that pop up and squirt water in their faces. The Pixies come home, finally, with all kinds of trinkets from their travels to decorate their tree houses with.

"How long did it take you to make this book?" I ask Beatrice, holding up a copy of *The Pixies Abroad*.

She takes it into her crimped hands. "Oh," she says. She adjusts her glasses and starts to turn the pages slow, chuckling at the Pixies' antics. "This is a long one," she says.

That doesn't answer my question. Unless she means it took longer than usual to make this one. "How long does one book usually take?" I ask.

Beatrice sighs. "A year or two," she says.

"A year?" I say. I don't have a whole year to do this. And I can't even draw yet. I ask Beatrice to draw a couple Pixies for me. It might be stupid, but I'm thinking if I can see the motions her hand makes, or what part she draws first, I'll be able to do it myself. I figure it's got to be just like learning a few chords on the guitar. Once you've done that, you have the whole world of rock 'n' roll at your fingertips. Nothing to it, really. Although I never quite managed to do that either.

Beatrice picks up a pencil and draws what I think is half the head of a Pixie, then comes down into an arm, maybe. Without lifting her hand from the page, she goes down the body, curves back out down one leg and stops. When Beatrice holds a pencil, you can see how holding it the way she did for years and years has to do with the way her fingers are crooked on her right hand. Curved in, like they were always pressing against this drafting board. She abandons the first squiggle and starts over, doing almost the exact same thing right next to it. All the sudden she throws the pencil down.

"Poo," she says. "What time is it? I can't do this now." She picks up the book I'd taken out and opens it on her lap.

I pull the paper a little closer and study the squiggles. They might not be budding Pixies at all, actually. To be honest, they look more like a couple of messy question marks in the middle of the paper. I try a few myself, not drawing in the hesitating, sketchy way I usually do, but keeping the pencil down to the paper, moving it like I have a purpose. Like I'm confident of what I'm doing, the way Beatrice seemed at first.

She's still sitting next to me. She makes a snuffling sound and I think she's laughing at my drawings. But when I look, she's bent over the open Pixies book with her hand over her mouth. Her face is all red. A droplet falls from her cheek and makes a faint tap when it lands on a page of frolicking Pixies.

"Oh, come on, don't," I say. I put my hand on Beatrice's shoulder and feel her little bones vibrating with grief. Another sob comes out of her and she makes another damp snuffling sound. She takes off her glasses, puts them on the drafting board and they slide to the floor. She rubs her cheeks, which are all wet now.

"I don't want to see anymore," she says.

As the book slides between her legs, folding itself shut and plunking on the floor, I hear a car pull up out front. I've got my arm around Beatrice and I'm trying to tell her it'll be all right when there's a sound like somebody rapping a gavel on the door. The screen door thwaps. Then there's Maylene's voice going, Hello? Mother? Hello?

She's startled when she sees me. Jerks her head and steps backward like somebody hit her on the forehead. Then she demands to know what I'm doing there. I ask her the same thing right back. Maylene's wearing a suit that makes her look like some kind of blow-dried mob boss. She says she and Beatrice have an appointment today.

"What for?" I ask.

Maylene gets real exasperated, slapping her hands against her thighs and acting like I'm so dense, saying can't I understand Beatrice needs periodic evaluations?

Well, don't get your panties all in a bunch, I tell her. I'm not staying home today to try and get in the way of any periodic evaluations. But after they leave I think something fishy is going on, I can tell. I'm not sure, but I think last time Maylene kidnapped Beatrice she used that same excuse. Like how often is periodic?

Either way, what it comes down to is I'm left alone here in the house. The wood around the windows makes cracking sounds once in a while as the sun gets higher. It gets hotter and hotter and I'm sweating over the drafting board, getting more and more frustrated by my sucky drawings until I snap my pencil in half and run all the way down to the pond and jump in. After all, I'm supposed to be playing hooky today. The water helps some, but I really don't feel like spending much time down here anymore. I swing off the rope, splash around and do the backstroke for a while. But I feel like a kid at the school playground after everybody else has gone home, commandeering the jungle gym with his imaginary friends, trying to convince himself that he's having a good time. That he doesn't mind being all alone.

The party Sheila invited me to is in Mt. Adams, this mini version of the yuppie district they have in real cities. If you want to be a big rebel in the Nasty, by going ahead and not having kids and not living in the burbs, you can come here where people in their thirties still wear the name of the college they went to on their sweater. Basically you're just on a campus that's got townhouses instead of regular dorms.

Mary-Beth, the woman whose townhouse we go into, seems to be under the impression that Sheila goes by the name "Girl," because as soon as she opens the door, she's all, Hey girl, Lookin' good girl, So tell me what's new girl. It's getting real windy outside, and it feels like we get blown in the front door. It slams shut behind us so we're sealed in the air conditioning. Mary-Beth shows us the other people, puts glasses of wine in our hands and doesn't bother us much after that. You can tell Mary-Beth is trying really hard to express her individuality with how she decorates her place because it looks just exactly like one of those boutiques you see in the mall. Sun-frame mirrors, curlicue candle holders, quirky picture frames, potpourri and polished rocks—the whole nine yards.

Well, everybody from Sheila's ski club brought a friend and it quickly turns into one of those real stiff, So-what-do-you-do? parties. All the sudden I notice this complete slob standing against the wall, holding a glass of wine like he's not sure what to do with it. It's me. Reflected in a mirror with a wide, curvilinear silver frame set with rhinestones or whatever. My un-tucked t-shirt is a little too long, my jeans are kind of frayed, not especially clean, and I have on a pair of old canvas sneakers. To make matters worse, I see, as I take a gulp from my glass—I'm drinking wine?—that I have a red rash along the insides of my forearms where I got all scratched up because we were planting junipers today. Looks like some terrible disease. Speaking of which, I have a few white bubbles of poison ivy erupting in the red Vs between my fingers. I start trying to keep my fingers closed like I have invisible mittens on. I rub my knuckles together a little now and then for the itching. But there's no hiding the black rims on all my fingernails. Oh, hell with it. Might as well just scratch my balls, where I have poison ivy too, right in front of everybody.

What are you supposed to do? I mean, is there some way to dress nice without turning into some version of the dick-faced guy who's obviously banging the Mary-Beth person, walking around the townhouse in a tight turtleneck sweater with a sports jacket over top of it? (I guess he knows how overly effective Mary-Beth's AC is.) Or—like this doughy dweeb in the circle of people I'm sort of talking to—wearing a button-down shirt tucked into pleated shorts with a belt and penny loafers? If there is, nobody told me about it.

The Heart of It All

This guy is telling everybody he's a sultan. I look around to see if I'm the only one who thinks he's crazy till he says it again and I realize he's saying consultant. But I never catch on to what it is he consults about. Everybody else seems to know already, so I'm not going to go and ask, and make myself look stupider than I already am. We're all standing in little circles, even though there's plenty of furniture around. I guess most of these folks have been sitting all day, but the leather recliner is looking real good to me. Or even the candy-striped couch.

This woman with fake blond hair, who says she's in marketing, talks about networking, liaisons, streamlining and coordinating, but pretty soon she lets it slip that what she does is she works for Proctor & Gamble. She seems to hit it off with the guy who does marketing for one of the other awful corporations in town and they both know some other guy who's in personnel at his company. So our circle is relieved of them.

A guy who wears rectangular glasses seems real proud of being a systems analyst because he talks about it awfully loud. But no matter how much he says, I can't get any clearer idea what he does than I got from the penny-loafered consultant. The systems analyst turns out to be one of these FYI enthusiasts. He talks about the free flow of information, which he seems to think is the solution to all the world's problems. He also seems to believe it's virtuous to learn all kinds of random bits of information about all different subjects. At one point he says that it's fascinating how the internet is changing the day-to-day world.

I don't say anything because I'm not so familiar with it, but as far as I can tell the internet isn't anything more than a television with a phone line attached. You know? I mean really. Basically, I'm standing here trying to keep a pleasant look on my face like I'm some blissed-out deaf person. Mary-Beth is banging around the kitchen with some other woman, supposedly getting dinner ready. It's a dinner party.

The systems analyst asks what I do. The way I look at it, what I "do" is I take care of Beatrice. But you can't go around telling people what you do is you're a caregiver for your grandmother. No way would they have any respect for you at all. Might as well tell them you deface billboards. But when I say landscaping, it's the first thing anybody has said that brings the analyst up short.

I can see now it's a real unsophisticated way to make a living. So to let them know I don't just mow lawns at least, I tell them we mostly do "installation," by which I mean putting plants in holes in the ground. I tell them we do commercial as well as residential and that we work with a variety of "plant material," which is what landscapers like Jim like to call them instead of just "plants." It sounds a lot spiffier.

They're like a modern Laurel and Hardy, these two. The systems guy is real scrawny and always has to push at the rectangles that keep sliding down his nose. The consultant is big and flabby with a goatee he starts stroking while I talk.

"You know," the consultant says, "sometimes I really feel like just going out and getting a blue-collar job like that. Working with my hands."

"Well, the novelty wears off pretty quick," I tell him. From the looks of his tender, pudgy hands, it probably wouldn't be such a great idea anyway. But he gets a look that makes me feel like I've been rude, so I add, "But we're always hiring, that's for sure." Then I drain my glass to have an excuse to get away from these guys.

I go in the kitchen and ask Mary-Beth if she needs any help. She's been left alone in here. Oh no, no, no, she says. Then I ask if she's got any beer or anything. She says of course and starts apologizing for not offering it before, I guess since it's pretty obvious from looking at me that I'm not the wine type. It's lighter beer than I'd like, what she gives me, but it'll do. When Mary-Beth says she has to go to the bathroom and I'm alone, I chug the beer right quick and open another so I'll be able to face that living room again.

When it comes down to it, I think I really don't like young people that much. They don't seem to realize anything. Like how dead we're all going to be pretty soon. All they do is show off for each other. They go around talking about themselves like they're the first person who ever walked around in shoes or whatever. Unless, that is, they're really young, I mean like little kids, and aren't addicted to facts yet. You can spend all day with a little kid you just met, hunting for hefilumps and woosels and you get along just great. They never start going, "Well now, see here. I've looked into this matter and my research has shown that neither hefilumps nor woosels exist, and therefore, if my calculations are correct, cannot be hunted."

There's got to be some certain age where a person all the sudden turns into a pretentious bore. And after that there's hardly ever any going back. That's why at a party like this one, I always feel like blowing my brains out all over the wall. But instead, I usually start looking at people, trying to figure out what each of them is going to look like when they're old. Take the consultant, for instance, when he's so fat his face and neck have become one. I try to picture his expression as he gasps for air through the hole in his gray goatee, right before he kicks the bucket.

Sheila comes over and puts her hand on my arm. I noticed it a little on the drive over here because she's wearing a sleeveless blouse—her arms look like a landscaper's. I mean, she must spend a lot of time in the weight room at some gym. "See that woman out on the veranda?" she asks, pointing out through the sliding glass doors. "That's Holly. She just got divorced recently."

"Oh," I say. This isn't my fault and I don't know why it's the first thing you'd say about somebody.

"Come on, I want to introduce you." Sheila starts pulling me along.

"Wait a second," I say. I down the rest of my beer and help myself to another as we go through the kitchen. I don't get these people who can just have two or three drinks. If I have two beers, I'm going to have about twelve. That's all there is to it.

Mary-Beth is still constructing this fabled dinner, but it's been so long I wonder if it's really going to happen. It means having to leave the air conditioning, but Sheila and I go through the sliding doors and Holly rouses herself from where she's leaning on the iron railing. She has chocolatey hair, kind of how Carla's was in the winter time. Holly is pale and cute like a little girl. I'm pretty used to it, but still, sometimes when I meet people my age or younger who are divorced, I wonder, like how did you get all that done already? I felt the same way growing up around here. By eighteen, nineteen, a lot of people were getting engaged.

"Oh, I just remembered I was going to do the salad," Sheila says, after she introduces us. "Excuse me." She goes back inside.

It's really gusting up out here. Dark clouds are racing in and the leaves on the trees across the street are standing up and showing their white underbellies. From where we're standing you can see across the muddy Ohio River to Kentucky. It's sort of nice because Newport and Covington are hardly anything. So if you squint, you can pretend you're still in some little 1800s steamboat stop.

I say something about how maybe the rain will give us a break from the humidity.

"Mmm," says Holly, looking out at the trees tossing around. Strands of hair blow across her face and she pulls them away and tucks them back behind a round little ear. "I love this weather," she says.

"Weather," I say. I put on my old pirate voice. "Arrr. This isn't no weather at all. When I sailed around Cape Horn in a raging hurricane, now that was *weather*."

Holly looks at me and smiles a tiny bit, kind of confused, then takes a sip of her wine. I consider climbing onto the railing, jumping off and splattering myself all over the parking lot below us. Holly gets a look on her face like I did just that, for a second, after I light up a cigarette. Oh well, who gives a shit? Like I'm retarded, I hold the pack out to offer her one, which seems like adding the one insult that can make up for the injury. Or maybe I just have a good buzz on by now.

The Heart of It All

Holly asks me the do question and when I say landscaping, she says, "Oh, that's interesting." Then she gets wrinkles between her eyebrows while she tries to imagine some way this might actually be interesting.

"Yeah I get to play with plants all day," I say. "Liriope and arborvitae, cedar and poplar. The xylem and the phloem. It's great stuff." I slur the last few words, which is okay, because it stops me from saying something really stupid about holly trees. I take a swig from my beer bottle like some kind of barbarian. "So what do you do?" I ask. And right away I'm sorry I did because she says she's a designer. Where does that leave you? I mean, there are designs of pretty much everything.

Luckily, Mary-Beth sticks her silly head out the door soon enough and tells us it's time for dinner. I'm just joshing her when I say, but it's still not even eleven o'clock yet. But she doesn't seem to find that funny. When we come in, I see Sheila talking to the marketing people. In order to laugh, she tilts her face toward the ceiling and shakes her head a little like she's rinsing out her hair in the shower. The thunder starts booming as we sit down around the table and I realize these are exactly the people Carla and I always made fun of. If she was here, I bet she'd—no, what are you thinking? She wouldn't ever be caught dead at some corny Mt. Adams dinner party.

Holly's in the chair next to me and across from me is this guy who keeps smiling and sticking his chin out at the same time. Then, every time, he glances over at the bleach-blond marketing woman. You can almost taste how good it would feel if your fist connected with his jaw right when he's doing one of these poses.

It's only pasta that took Mary-Beth all this time, but she got a lot of pieces of salad mixed up in it. Apparently she spilled some bird food in it too because there are these little seeds you keep crunching on every so often.

The systems analyst is still talking real loud about writing code and it dawns on me what the fucker does. It's some computer shit. He's pretending to be talking to the woman next to him, but he's so loud you can tell he wants the whole table listening. My mind starts filling up with all that computer jargon. He's talking about this new company he's working at, what a bunch of dimwits these folks are. At one point he says, "And then I realized, these people wouldn't know the difference between C+ and Java."

"Tell me about it, it's the worst," I say, a little too loud. Everybody looks at me because it's the first thing I've said since we sat down. "It's like this morning—I booted up and accessed my vehicle. First thing, we had to download a couple tons of manure. So then after that I have to interface with a member of our multicultural staff. I say, 'Vamos a plantar estas cosas aquí.' And he says to me, 'Eh, pendejo, tengo ojos en la cara.'"

Well, that went over like a turd in the punch bowl. Nobody even cracks a smile. Sheila is staring at me in a way I know she'd be giving me the hand-slitting-throat signal if the other people couldn't see her.

"It's a communication problem is what it comes down to," I say, like to wrap up. I take a swig of beer. I'm the only one not drinking wine. I don't really care that I just killed the conversation dead. Holly seems to be leaning away from me like she's afraid I might get violent. I might, who knows? Then there's a thunder clap and the first flash of lightning and everybody has that to start talking about. I tip back in my chair so I can see through the kitchen and try to figure how much rain is coming down. I pray for rain every morning, so we can get off work early. So now, when it does me no good, is when it comes down. It's gotten dark outside, but I can see a curtain of rain in the light that's on the balcony. Then Mary-Beth says she's sorry but she'd rather I didn't lean back like that because these chairs are quite delicate, by which I can tell she means expensive.

When I let myself drop back to the table, I glance at Holly, who's talking to the guy on the other side of her. I only realize because now it's so obvious, it was supposed to be a set-up, me and her. I can easily picture Sheila and Mary-Beth getting their heads together: "Let's set Holly up with the landscaper. Wouldn't that be cute?" They probably even orchestrated that whole Romeo and Juliet scene on the balcony too. Guess I fucked up my part pretty bad.

When dinner finally ends, we all go out to go to a shiny yuppie bar. The rain has let up already but the wind is still real strong. After a couple shots and a few more beers, I start asking people, Which are the best slopes in the Nasty? Ohio's highest peak is actually a heap of garbage in a landfill not far north of here—have you made a trip up there yet? You think we'll get some nice powder on Mt. Adams this year? It'd be pretty cool to ski right straight down this hill except you'd land on Central Parkway and there isn't a chair lift to get back.

"We're planning a trip to Vail this year," the sultan lets me know, then rotates his thick head away from me and starts talking to somebody else. I doubt they'd let me in their club even if I could afford the dues. That's okay. I'm just sitting here talking to nobody now, watching the TV over the bar, waiting for my cousin to take me home. Everybody else jabbers on. Somebody puts "Wild Horses" on the juke box and I have to watch the TV real hard and keep swallowing beer to wash down the lump that keeps coming up in my throat.

Carla would have come over, put her arm on my shoulder, taken a drag from my cigarette, put it back in my mouth, then said, "These people are dorks. C'mon, let's blow this popsicle stand."

At first, Sheila's so pissed she can't say anything when we get in the car. The roads are totally dry already from the heat and the wind. After a couple miles, Sheila says, "Why do you hate everything?"

"I don't hate everything," I say. "I just hate stuff that sucks."

"You know, John, you really need to grow up."

"Not if I can help it," I say. I know she's right though. I really got to quit it. I mean shit, I'm going to be forty. Not for ten years, but still.

"I think you'd feel better about yourself if you didn't do that stupid job. You don't have to, you know. Other people go back to school. Other people find work they enjoy."

"Other people don't have criminal records." Whoops. It just sort of hiccupped out of me like that. And now Sheila's going, What do you mean, what do you mean, oh my God, John, what happened?

"It was a mistake," I say. "I mean, I did it on accident." My tongue won't cooperate. "I didn't even do it, really. All I know is, one minute you're in a bar swapping stories with some guy and complaining about how broke you are, and the next thing you know you wake up and this other guy in the bunk above you has these gang symbols tattooed all over his neck and you're waiting to go on work release."

I remember more than that actually, but not much. I'm not about to tell Sheila the whole thing about how I was supposed to be the getaway driver, which was kind of a joke because I couldn't even really walk, I was so shitfaced. I don't remember how I got there, but I remember sitting in the driver's seat, looking through the windshield like I was just waking up. Through the smeared glass doors of a convenience store we'd parked in front of, I saw this greasy looking guy robbing the place. If I'd known he had a gun on him before that, no way I would have gotten in a car with him. Next thing, the greasy guy's in the passenger seat, his face right in mine yelling, "Drive motherfucker!"

From what they said in court, it seems I stepped on the gas, backed up fast and slammed right into a dumpster. Then, trying to get out of the parking lot, the cop who was testifying said I crashed right into his cruiser, already arriving at the scene because he was parked at a strip mall across the street when the robbery happened. And when they pulled me out of the car I vomited all over the arresting officer. He left out the part about how right after that he bashed me on the noggin with his nightstick, because that huge lump didn't grow there by itself, I don't think.

In court, I remember the owner of the store we'd hit, how he glared at me like he wanted to kill me with his bare hands. I'll never forget that determined, tiny, brown man, who must have worked his ass off to get to this country and was working his ass off now in that crappy little store. I honestly wished the judge would let the poor guy do his worst to me while I was cuffed, because I knew right then I was the scum of the earth. All the privilege and opportunity I had simply been born with, and here I was trying to take the curried lamb or whatever out the mouths of the seven little kids he probably had living in his back room. I mean, Jesus Christ, it really makes you wonder just what in the hell is the world coming to.

By the time she drops me off, Sheila's gotten herself all upset. "Let me know if there's anything I can do," she says, as I'm getting out of her car, a little unsteady. Must be the strong wind that's still gusting.

"You could come over and give Beatrice her baths," I say. "That's the one thing I can't seem to get comfortable with."

Sheila bites her lower lip. I can understand she doesn't actually want to; it was good enough of her to ask. "I don't think you have to worry about taking care of Grandma for much longer," she says.

I burp in the wind. I sway in the breeze. I have no idea what she's talking about.

"Mom's going to put her in a home soon," Sheila says.

"Nah," I say. "I won't let her."

"I don't think you're going to have any say in the matter. And besides, Mom said Grandma's gotten to a stage where she needs professional care."

"Maylene's smokin' crack," I say. "There's no good reason Beatrice's gotta be locked up someplace. Maylene should just leave us alone."

Forgetting that I already ruined it, Sheila tells me good night. And drives off. I go in and call Gary and wake him up.

"It's been raining, dude. We can't paint anything," he says.

"The roads are dry. I don't wanna do billboards tonight anyways. I gotta write to my congressman."

One time, many moons ago, Gary and I found one of those white canes with red on one end that blind people use. Gary had just been fired from a job, after less than a week, as a security guard at a shopping mall. So he put on a pair of dark glasses and I drove him out there. He went into practically every shop, tapping his cane around, waving his hands in front of him and knocking all the merchandise off every shelf he could, bumping into displays of dishes, toy trucks, books or whatever. With his hip like it was a mistake, or just kicking them so they toppled over. By the time the store staff caught up with him he'd usually pretty much trashed the place. Then, while they were leading him out the door, he'd rub his hands all over one of their faces, going, "Zigfried? Zigfried?" It was about the funniest thing you ever saw in your life. Whenever it looked like he might get in trouble with a security guard, I'd run into the store saying I was looking for my poor blind brother.

Since then, if either one of us ever wanted to do a revenge thing and needed some kind of help, but the other didn't want to worry about having to take the fall, we'd say, You can do this one blind. Which meant you didn't have to know anything specific about what the other was going to do. It doesn't make perfect sense. But it could keep you out of trouble if it came down to your word in a court of law. But I'm in a pretty bad mood from that yuppie party and I accidentally spill some of the beans while we're on the drive out.

"Are you sure you really wanna do this?" Gary says, while we're driving out to Heighberger's neck of the woods. "You're plastered, man."

"Course," I say. "What do you expect? You try drinkin' a couple glasses of wine and a dozen beers without getting plastered."

Heighberger's got a colossal colonial out here in Anderson Township. There's a blacktop circular drive, so I need a can of white. I know what you're really supposed to do is write a letter to your congressman. But this is way more direct. Besides, what I have to say isn't even a whole sentence. You wouldn't want to waste the paper and stamp.

"Don't do this," Gary says, grabbing my arm as I get out of the car. "They probably have kids and they'll have to see that shit in the morning."

I jerk my arm away. "Well, maybe daddy'll have to explain to them what he's got against the caribou that're just trying to live peaceful up there in the north latitudes."

Real big, I paint, BEGIN DRILLING HERE on the driveway, then make a long arrow going down to a big X by the front door.

8

In the morning, I'm trying to make myself conscious with a big bowl of coffee in the front room. I look out the window at the haze of humidity and listen to the cicadas making their long buzzing that sounds like an oven timer going off. It's a mating thing. Pretty disgusting. I mean, what if I just stood there yelling at the top of my lungs every time I got horny? Earlier in the week, I kept finding the little dry husks of the shed cicada bodies, still clinging to tree branches. There was one right on the porch steps. They get to just fly off to some new place in their new bodies. Must be nice.

Beatrice is quietly discussing something with Stanley in the kitchen. Sheila calls and tells me she's sorry about last night. Again, she points out that I must be under a lot of stress, taking care of Beatrice. I say that's a crock.

"But I really do think you should figure out a career to pursue," she says. "You'll be so much happier."

"Career?" I say. "Shit. I'd be happier if Ryan just got a thatcher that works. You should've seen how long it took me to do a tiny lawn renovation last week with this crummy thing conking out on me every two minutes."

"See, you have to think bigger than that, John. You seem interested in environmental issues. Wouldn't you rather do work where you can influence policy?"

"Yeah, I was working on that last night, actually. Listen, what's with all this concern all a sudden?" She wants to know what I mean. "You know what I mean," I say. "Not a peep out of you all summer and then in one weekend you're trying to get my social life and professional life all up to speed."

Sheila starts warbling about busyness and I hear a sickening thump in the kitchen and Beatrice say, "Oh!" Gotta go, I say, hang up and rush into the other room. Beatrice is holding onto a chair, pulling herself up off the kitchen floor. I help her up into the chair and just miss stepping on her glasses. She seems surprised by the fall, but not hurt.

"What happened?" I ask.

"What time is it?" she asks. Her cheeks are flushed with embarrassment.

"Eleven," I say. "What happened?"

"I was talking to him," she says and her eyes get moist. "I was talking—" She sniffles and rubs that turned-up little Pixie nose. "I could use a tricycle," she says.

I get her a tissue from a box on the counter and she blows her nose. She blows it for longer than she needs to, and looks at me over top of the tissue with big bloodshot eyes. The bottom lids sag down so the wet pink part looks vulnerable. Also, there are these spaces over the top of her eyelids like the eyeballs are gradually sinking down in her skull.

"I was talking to him," she says. "And I got out of my chair. I was going to get something to drink. I got up and I put my hand out to steady myself on his arm." She drops her hands in her lap and starts sobbing. Uncontrollable.

Not sure if she's going to accept this, I pull a chair up next to her and put my arms around her. But she does. She plops her skinny arms right up on my shoulders like she's throwing them over a life raft and sobs into my chest. I can feel her tears making my t-shirt damp.

"He wasn't there," she keeps saying. "He wasn't there." I know just how she feels, so I hug her until she stops crying and I talk her into playing gin rummy for a little while. I keep a pack of cards on top of the refrigerator. We played all the time when I was a kid and she was impossible to beat. But now she gets distracted so easily I find myself having to let her win a game now and then. We play for about an hour and she seems to get back to at least a stable, if not a happy, mood.

Later in the afternoon, I'm reading in the living room when Beatrice comes in and does the weirdest thing I've seen her do yet. She comes up to the other armchair. It looks like she's going to sit in it. But she walks around behind it, then starts climbing over the back of it. It almost tips over, so I go to help. First I have to convince her that she doesn't have to climb over the back of it, that she can come around the front of it. I demonstrate sitting in the chair for her. She watches me suspiciously and mutters, "Dangerous, backwards," when I sit down. Then I have to practically hold her in front of the chair, ask her to sit, and sort of lower her down. "I'm okay, I'm okay," she says, getting a little huffy.

This isn't good. In fact it's scary as hell. In my mind, I start to review some of the shit that's been going down around here for the last couple weeks. There have been more incidents like with the eggs lately—pouring milk next to the glass instead of into it, seeming to set a cup down on the counter when the counter is two feet from where Beatrice lets go of the cup. Stuff like that. And now this thing with the chair.

Letting her keep going up and down stairs is probably a bad idea. I have a day-mare of Beatrice lying at the foot of the stairs for several hours with a busted hip, while I'm off doing Ryan Rinckel's dirty work. You know, they really ought to think more about old people when they're designing houses and cars and shit.

So I spend the rest of the day rearranging furniture and setting up Beatrice's bed in the living room and moving all her stuff from the upstairs bathroom to the one down here. All while I'm doing it, Beatrice keeps asking me if we're expecting company.

"Is there going to be a party?" she asks. "Is it Christmas?"

The Heart of It All

Sure. I tell her yes to all these things and after a while it starts to feel like it is. I mean, a special occasion at least. I put on the radio station she likes, the one that plays the songs from when swing was king, and she starts rearranging some of the kick-knacks on the bookshelves and tables. I find some wide red ribbons to tie to the end of the banister and thumbtack to the opposite wall at the bottom of the stairs. I tell Beatrice she doesn't have to go up them anymore. We have a pretty good time together, getting ready for this party that's never coming.

There's storm damage. Our customers are all bent out of shape about that. Bunch of them called Ryan over the weekend. Broken limbs hanging down, strewn all over the yard. Absolute chaos. To look at it, you might go so far as think that to destroy herself is nature's way. And if you don't stop there, you might go on to wonder about human nature. Very unsettling for some folks.

So Carlos and yet another new guy, Miguel, and I are getting rid of as much of the evidence of the storm as we can this morning. It was a pretty long weekend for me and I'm feeling a little floaty. Beatrice was up a couple of times wandering around last night. We had another midnight breakfast.

Which is maybe why, when I give Carlos the pole pruner and show him the broken, dangling limbs that have to come down, I assume he knows what he's doing. When you're cutting big branches, you have to make two cuts on the limb a foot or so out from the trunk—one on top of the branch, cutting about halfway through the limb, and one on the underside of the branch a few inches away from that. That way your branch comes off clean. Then you can go ahead and cut off the stub that's left, right at the collar. If you just make one cut next to the trunk, when the branch comes down it can strip a big piece of bark down the trunk and leave an awful wound. Maybe even end up killing the tree.

I'm cutting up a tree that came completely down in the storm. Cutting it into sections so we can throw the pieces of trunk in the truck and the branches in the chipper. I'm trying to concentrate on holding the hollering chainsaw steady, because I know that due to the unsteady state I'm in I'm liable to find myself on one leg, slowly tipping over, before I realize I've cut the other one off below the knee. I hear a shout, and when I look around, sure enough, this big beech tree looks like a half-peeled banana and Carlos is sprawled on the ground with the pole pruner and the broken limb on either side of him.

He bounces up quick like he did after he went flying off the truck that time on the first day. But then he starts kind of stumbling around holding his hand over his face. When I get over to him there's blood soaking his mustache and running over his chin.

"Siéntate, siéntate," I tell him, and get him sitting down even though he doesn't want to be. I'm pretty sure it isn't broken, but the blood is just gushing out of Carlos's nose. Miguel gives him a handkerchief to hold over it and I get him to tilt his head back.

Sheila was giving me shit the other night about not having health insurance, but Christ—this is a whole other story. Carlos can't go to a hospital. He doesn't have any money; he sends it all to his family in Mexico and he doesn't know anybody except these other illegal guys who aren't going to be able to help him much. Carlos's eyes keep going from the sky, to me, over to Miguel. You can tell his pride is hurt more than anything else.

But I'm realizing how delicate this guy is. I've seen him lift big stones, and clean-and-jerk wheelbarrows full of rocks and dirt that had to weigh as much as he does, onto the half-raised lift on the back of the truck. But his forearms are about the size of Beatrice's. And here he is so far from home in a hostile country where all this machinery and falling branches can maim him and he's in constant danger of being arrested.

The Heart of It All

He's only twenty-six. In some little pueblo, in an adobe hut or whatever, he's got a wife who must be worried sick about him. Probably a worried mom, too, in a neighboring hut. And he's got two kids, he told me that much. How come we don't help these people?

Now I can see from how Carlos is glancing nervously over at the tree he disfigured that he's afraid he might lose his job. On top of all the other shit.

"Señor Estúpido," I say, just to let him know not to worry. "Mucho pendejo, mucho pendejo." And I shake my head and make a little clicking sound with my tongue, like, "What the heck are we gonna do with you?" He tries and get up to get back to work. But I tell him to sit back down and stay put for at least diez minutos. After a while his nose stops bleeding and by lunchtime he's joking around again, though his nose has a bump on it that looks uncomfortable. I'm glad he's better because the commercial job we have in the afternoon I want to get over with as quick as possible.

Parking lot landscaping is about the worst. What we have to do this afternoon is pull out these dead boxwoods on all the little beds scattered around out in front of this grocery store and replace them with spirea that are also going to die. The problem isn't the plants, it's that the soil here is crap. No nutrients in it.

So we're ripping out boxwoods and trying to watch we don't get run down—by aggravated shoppers who glare at us like we're doing something criminal, from inside their air-conditioned cocoons-on-wheels, while we gasp and wipe the dripping sweat from our faces onto our grimy RR t-shirts—when I see Carla. Walking right across the parking lot. Or another woman who's impersonating Carla's graceful, confident stride and imitating her curves. Only she's got shoulder-length reddish hair. But she's even trying to mimic Carla's straight nose and her thin but expressive lips.

I leave my shovel standing in a hole. "Voy a comprar una bebida," I tell Carlos, who's nose is more swollen and changed color a little. He starts to give me a few crumpled bills to get pops for him and Miguel. I tell him to keep his poco dinero. I'll treat.

It's getting to be the end of the summer, but still it's almost ninety degrees and in this blacktop parking lot it's like walking around on a huge frying pan. I follow the woman as she gets a cart and starts moving slow down the aisles. Carla would never put in her cart this big box of disposable diapers, which I know she knows is what's overflowing the landfills. Besides, Carla doesn't have kids. And Carla doesn't wear these black stretchy work-out shorts either, even though you've got to admit they sure look good on her thighs.

The lady turns and gives me the sharp, "Fuck off" look she'd give any sweaty creep covered in topsoil, standing too close to her in the grocery store and obviously not shopping.

"John?" she says, kind of blinking—I think mainly because the bangs, which she never had before, come right down and hit her eyelids.

"Hey," I say stupidly. Like I'm always running into her in the paper goods aisle.

She laughs, and it's genuine. Her old laugh is coming out of this new woman who has possessed Carla. "Well, what the hell?" she says. "Did you just sprout up out of the ground? And what are you doing here? Last I heard, you were out West."

She looks incredible, even wearing makeup, which she must have just started doing. She looks like the kind of woman I'd see on the street and say, Wow. There goes a woman who'd never have anything to do with me. Guess I know that for sure now.

"Beatrice has Alzheimer's," I say. "I'm sort of taking care of her." This is pathetic. I've pictured a hundred thousand times what I'd be like when I finally saw Carla again and I wasn't ever anything near this. Like some dirty bum following her around the grocery store, talking about his grandmother.

"Oh, I was so sorry to hear about that," Carla says. "Sheila told me." Her eyes go down for a second and that's when I notice her hands on the handle of the shopping cart, the long-fingered, slightly muscular hands I've held in mine so many times. And I see the ring.

"Beatrice is such a sweet, wonderful lady," Carla says.

I never felt so much like puking, screaming, shitting, collapsing on my knees and crying all at once. I guess it's easy for Carla to see I'm having trouble.

"You should come over for dinner some time," Carla says. "You have to meet Jeremy. He's such a trip."

Jeremy. So she married a Jeremy, of all the dumb stupid-ass names in the whole wide world.

"The other day," says Carla, "I told him a joke and he says 'Mom, you're such a Canadian.' If you ask him what he wants to be when he grows up he says a triceratops."

"So..." I say, slow, like my batteries are dying, "that means... there's..."

"Two. Right," Carla says. She waves a hand at the box of diapers. "Ann is the new addition. Jeremy's four now." She cocks her head. "Didn't Sheila tell you this? I've spoken with her fairly often. She came to our wedding. I wanted to send you an invite, but she didn't know exactly where you were at the time."

Our wedding? No, no, no. Wait a minute. She married somebody else. That much is clear. But this is all wrong. Carla's treating me like Sheila might treat some good old pal she happened to be on a coed soccer team with for a couple seasons. Not like the love of her life.

She talks a little bit longer and it turns out it's Brad. I can't believe she actually stood at an altar with that stuffed piece of shit. In front of a priest. It occurs to me some members of our old drinking crowd were probably best men and rice throwers and so on. What a cliché scary movie scenario. Look at how pretty they all are in their matching dresses—the maids of horror!

I tell the new Carla I'd better get back to work.

She says, "Really, we should have you over for dinner." She says she'll call me at Beatrice's.

Yeah, right. I walk back out into the heat, thinking, I'm sure that will happen. I can just see it: Oh, that's okay Brad, let me carve the roast—whoops!—oh shit, that was your hand I held down on the platter and chopped right off. Darn! Here, hold this napkin over the stump while I—oh, no—there I go again! I'm stabbing you repeatedly in the chest! Gosh, I really can be a total klutz sometimes! Blood is splattering all over the walls, splashing on the carpet as you flail around now. Stop screaming like that, please, can't you see you're upsetting the children? So calm down. That's better. Sure, lie down. What're you doing now? Oh, that's all right Brad. It's your dinner party, you can die if you want to.

My shovel is still standing in the hole I left it in. Carlos stops working and looks at me like I just stepped off a spacecraft. What? What the hell? I mean, he's the alien. He holds out his arms.

"Eh, pendejo. Dónde están las bebidas?"

Well, I can't always be expected to remember every single little goddamn thing like pops, now can I? What the hell am I doing? Why am I here? Is this my real life? I'm digging a hole so deep I could bury a spirea plant in it, even though we haven't finished taking out all the boxwoods and it looks like we won't be able to start planting till tomorrow. I dig like my life depends on it while Carla comes out and loads her groceries into the back of... no way! It's an SUV. She beeps and waves as she's pulling out. I look up, wipe the sweat on my sleeve, smile and wave like I'm some landscaper. Yup, just doing my job here! Happy day!

Then I drop my shovel and run for the truck, yelling, "Vamos! Vamos!"

Carlos is confused but he drops his shovel too. By the time he swings open the door and hops in, the truck is already moving. "Qué pasó? Qué pasó?" he keeps saying. Miguel isn't going to make it. He was way on the other side of the lot. I yell at him that we'll be back, but I doubt if he hears me.

She can't live too far from here if this is where she gets her groceries. It's tricky. I have to stay back a ways because I don't want her to see me in her rearview mirror, but I don't want to lose sight of her. Luckily, I know the roads in this area like the back of my hand. We're not far from the farm.

All the sudden Carlos is squawking and pointing and I slam on the brakes. I'd been looking over the roofs of the cars about four ahead of us—this truck rides plenty high—to where Carla's is, so I didn't notice the van right in front of us had stopped. Our bumper stops probably an inch from the back of it. The license plate must have fallen off its screws because they have it hanging in the van's back window. And there it is, a little above the level of the hood of our truck, staring me in the face. "OHIO," in bold blue letters on the white plate, and under that in red, in a kind of handwriting that's I guess supposed to express enthusiasm, "*the heart of it all!*"

I follow Carla past a golf course that used to be a soy bean field, I think. No, it was woods. That's right, it was all woods here! Shit. We used to drive out this way together at night, past the woods, to a huge cornfield because there was no light pollution and we could see the stars better. We'd traipse out into the middle of the field and get stoned and look up at the stars and have sex, right there in the cornfield. Now Carla turns her SUV just after the goddamn golf course and goes up a ridge that used to be covered with trees but now features a subdivision of big bland houses that overlooks the golf course. I can't believe she's doing this. She's got to know I'm following. She's going to pull over to the side of the road (even though there's no side of the road, really, or sidewalks, here in what they've idiotically named Fox Chase Manor, though I think

Deforestation Subdivision would have been more apropos) get out of her SUV, walk over to my truck stopped right behind her and say, Ha, ha! Really had you going there for a minute, didn't I? C'mon. You didn't think I'd really be living in one of these cheesy places did you?

But she doesn't. Instead, she pulls into one of the hundred identical cement driveways and she and the SUV get swallowed by a three-car garage that shuts its mouth, leaving Carlos and me sitting in the idling truck a few doors down, staring. Knowing we've just witnessed a terrible, terrible crime.

"La chica?" he's saying. "Tu conoces? La chica bonita?"

"Sí, sí sí," I say. Thinking, Oh, sure, sure. The lost translation parrot in my head saying, Yeah, I know the pretty girl. I know the pretty girl. But of course it's not true. I don't know the pretty girl. Not at all. I have absofuckinglutely no idea who she is.

To turn the truck around, I back into somebody's driveway and hear the scrape of metal against metal. I look in the rearview as I pull back forward and see I bent a mailbox back on its stem. The door came open and the mailbox looks like a big mouth silently screaming at the sky.

9

So I skip work on Thursday because I feel like I need some daycare. But first off, early in the morning, I decide to go through the stack of mail. It's been piling up, but I have a system. I separate all the bills. I take the old stack of bills and throw them out unopened because the new ones will include the old charges. Then I stack all the bills neatly and put them on the window ledge were I keep them to open and pay later when I have more time. That frees me up to go flipping through magazines and clothes catalogs, blacking out the teeth of the models and giving them pointy beards, curly mustaches and eyeglasses.

On a whim, I open my latest bank statement and the final balance seems off, even though I only have a really vague notion how much should be in there. There's another envelope with the name of my bank. This one's got a letter and it says they apologize for the inconvenience, but they have not been able to process a check from Ryan Rinckel, Inc. but they're real on top of things here at this bank and they're following up on this matter they know must be of high concern for one of their valued customers, me. Well now I feel pretty important for a minute—I mean, at least I'm special to somebody quietly suffering behind a desk somewhere—till I realize exactly what this means.

I call the number they put on the letter, and after listening to recorded voices for five or ten minutes, decide no, what I'd like actually is to talk to a real live human being. I tell Beatrice we've got to go to the bank before daycare and she doesn't have any objections.

Like I said, Beatrice doesn't generally get paranoid. But all these people in the bank are making her real nervous. When I get in line, she goes over to one of the tables in the middle of the room where you can stand and endorse your checks or whatever. She keeps glancing suspiciously over at the tellers, stuffing her hip pockets with deposit slips till her pants are bulging with them. I go over and convince her to come stand in line with me.

I swear to God. You take off work, thinking you'll get a break from the reek of mulch and manure. But now this bank smells like the freaking port-a-potty at a swap meet. Beatrice hasn't asked me what time it is the whole ten minutes we've been in here, which is odd. That's her usual way of trying to get her bearings. But she can't keep still. She keeps shuffling around next to me so much I wonder if her feet are hurting her. Then she rips a fart that sounds like a tiny prop plane starting up.

She glances around to see if anybody's noticing. And they are. The suited fat man in front of us turns around, makes a lemon-sucking expression, flares his nostrils and turns his back again. Just looking down, I can see that Beatrice is carrying a load in her pants. Those aren't deposit slips in the back. Her face is getting red. She looks up at me and says, What, what? She knows. I tell her let's forget this, I can do it some other time. I hold her hand and lead her out the doors. I get her into the car and tell her, wait just a second, I'll be right back.

I saw the guy getting his fat ass out of his expensive sedan when we were pulling in the lot. So I go over to it and hawk a luger on the driver's side window, then go back to Beatrice. I probably should wait till he comes out and spit right in the fucker's face to teach him a lesson. Some people have no sense of decency. Did he think Beatrice shit her pants in public just to annoy him? I mean, couldn't he see how embarrassed she was? Besides which, she drew the groundbreaking children's books that were obviously wasted on him because he's grown up to be a total sell-out who thinks he's important because he stands around in a suit.

The Heart of It All

I put all the windows down for the ride back to the farm. I've got to get Beatrice cleaned up before daycare. There are so many cicadas shrieking outside, sometimes when you're driving along it sounds like one big insect is whirring along beside you. Beatrice keeps shifting around in her seat. Looks out the window, quieter than usual. I put my hand on hers. Even with how calloused my palms and fingers are from using a shovel all summer, I can feel the blue vein like a rubber earthworm that sticks out on the back of her hand.

"It's going to be okay," I say. But I know it's not.

Beatrice turns to look at me, a little guarded. "What is?" she asks.

"I don't know," I say, rubbing my eyes.

"It's going to be okay," she says. She pats my thigh since, after all, I'm the one crying.

We're late and we've missed exercises and choir practice. Everybody is seated around the tables now, working on different projects. I went to one of the other recitals this summer at an old folk's home. Beverly thought it went much better than the first one. She said everyone must have just been nervous at that first one at the hospital. I thought it went about the same, except Harvey didn't walk off the stage. And the staff seemed more like they thought it was a good thing.

Daycare is just like any other day job you ever get. When you first walk in the place, it seems like everybody is busy, efficiently doing all the different things that have to get done. Then after you've been there a little bit, you realize they're all doing completely random bullshit and nothing they could ever do here will ever matter to anybody. Not even themselves. But, of course, this is way better than any job because there's no hierarchy. An Alzheimer's victim treats you the same whether you've been in their lives for twenty years or twenty minutes.

Norm's sitting at the head of one of the tables and it looks like he's presiding over an important board meeting. Till you look a little closer and see that what they're doing is making paper flower chains to hang around the walls. Norm's scissors are lying on the table for now while he fills everybody else in on the importance of increasing rates of production.

Out the window I see Roger by himself, pacing back and forth in the yard like he does. I go out there and he greets me with his usual nod. Always looks like he's trying to refrain from saluting whenever he sees me.

"You know this fog today is reminding me of the Ardennes Offensive—were you there?"

I tell him I couldn't have been. He looks off, over the fence that goes around this yard to keep him and others from wandering out. Down the street I don't know what he sees. Advancing artillery maybe. It's not foggy exactly, just real hazy from the humidity. They mentioned a smog alert on the radio earlier.

"Well, you're lucky then," Roger says. "We couldn't see a goddamn thing. It was like pea soup. And the terrain wasn't much better—thick mud. And cold. God almighty, you'd have mud caked on your boots and cemented on with frost." I can kind of relate to this, I think. "Terrible," he goes on. "A few fellas, buddies of mine, lost toes to gangrene. We were up on the northern shoulder. Which regiment did you say you were with?"

"I was on leave," I say. "We had a death in the family."

"Oh," says Roger. He looks back over the fence, peering through the haze to the 1940s. Where he's still stuck in a muddy foxhole or whatever. His bridges back are all bombed to hell.

"You wanna come inside for a while?" I ask. "It looked like some folks were getting a card game together."

"No, no," he says on an upbeat, as he looks down at his geriatric shoes with the thick soft soles. "I'd rather get the air, keep my strength up. They could be shipping me out again any day now. You know how it is."

I stay to exchange a few more tidbits of small talk, then Roger winks at me as I turn to go back inside. He goes back to his pacing along the fence.

Beatrice, I'm glad to see, has gotten involved in a card game. Sometimes she isolates herself too much, spending her time just looking after Phil. He's sitting next to her now, stiff. Holds his cards out in front of his face, his mouth hanging open like he's shocked by what he sees on them. Beatrice puts her own hand down on the table, leans over, takes one of Phil's cards and puts it in the discard pile, gets another from the stack and puts it in his hand. Deidre draws a card but doesn't discard. Norm impatiently drums his fingers on the table and sighs heavily through his nose. I feel like I still owe him one for saving my ass when we got pulled over. I look around the room and notice Cliff and Mildred aren't here today.

"What're you playing?" I ask.

"Poker," Norm says.

"But not the stripping kind," says Virginia. I doubt she could unbind herself from the elaborate gown she's got on anyway.

"We're playing hearts," Beatrice says.

"I thought this was gin rummy," says Deidre. She pushes her glasses up her nose. They never seem to fit right since the time Norm knocked them off her face. She looks around the room. "Is there a rummy table?"

I should have known better than to ask. Some of them are holding five cards, some have eight. Some have cards laid down on the table with matching suits, some don't.

Out of nowhere, someone screams, "You took it!" A woman named Ellen gets up from one of the other tables. "I knew it!" she screams. It's Joanne she's yelling at. Poor Joanne cowers at first, then gets brave and tries to reach out to Ellen, who snaps her arm out of reach. "You're always stealing from me! You witch! Why do you hate me!"

"A pair of Jacks," says Norm calmly, putting his cards down for everybody to see. Nobody at this table except me even looked up when Ellen started her fit. It's almost like they know the same lightning can strike them at any second, so why bother about it? The only thing Joanne can do right now is to wait for the electrical charge to leave Ellen's body, then offer to help find whatever it is Ellen thinks she stole.

Beverly looks over from where she's standing on a chair, tacking a paper daisy chain up over the windows. She decides to let Joanne handle it. I think Beverly looks like a famous sculpture, standing up there in front of the windows. She's wearing a tight black jog-bra and hot pink short-shorts. And she's glistening with sweat, all over her arms and big round thighs. I wish! Actually, she's wearing a baggy white blouse and oversized khaki shorts that come down almost to her knees. Still, you can see her hips straining the khaki just below the belt. And you can see her bare white calves and the pink creases on the backs of her knees. Oh, that goddamn sassy little sexpot! Well, not little. Big sexpot. But what I wouldn't do to her!

And what's stopping me anyway? I mean, nobody ever says anything about how gross it is when a real successful man starts screwing some chick young enough to be his daughter. They still smile at him in public and shake his grubbing, groping hand. They seem to approve, even applaud what he does. Sacrifice the virgins to capitalism! Yahoo! So it only makes sense that a real unsuccessful man like me should hook up with a woman who's fifteen years older than he is.

She's just getting down from the chair now, admiring the festoons of paper flowers. Like it's anything to look at as long as her ass is still in the same room. I go over and ask, Where are Cliff and Mildred today? Totally innocent.

Bev gets a fretful look. "They aren't going to be coming, I'm afraid. Cliff finally decided to place her in assisted living."

The Heart of It All

Far as I'm concerned, if it's assisted, it can hardly be called living anymore. But no way in hell am I going to say that to Beverly. I say, Well, it's too bad, I'm sure going to miss them. And that's true. Beverly says we're all going to miss them, and I'm worried the conversation is going to dry right up and blow away. I say the daisy chain looks nice.

"I have other projects I'm excited about too," she says. "I think the hand-eye coordination is so important to maintain." We look over at one of the tables where they're still making the flower chains.

"As long as no one pokes an eye out," I say.

"Oh, dear." Beverly's round cheeks go slack. She touches my arm. I love when she does that. I could just sit in a room all day long while Bev touches my arm. "You know, I hadn't even thought of that," she says.

I say we could go sit with them and kind of supervise. That way we could take the scissors away from anybody whose hands seem a little too shaky. So we go and pull up chairs and take up scissors. We're sitting so close my knee is almost touching Bev's thigh. We talk about this and that while we cut flower chains with everybody else. Or they do. I cut something that looks more like a mangled orange snowflake. When I unfold it, I have a whole chain of mangled orange snowflakes.

Soon as I get up the nerve, I'm going to ask Beverly if she's busy for dinner on Saturday. Any second now. Just need the right moment. Then—it's true, there is a God, a sadistic God who tortures us for laughs—Joanne comes over, pulls up a chair and sits on Bev's other side.

Did Joanne sense, from the other side of the room, that I was about to make an unholy proposition? She steals all Beverly's attention, starts babbling some Bible shit. Now it hits me. I have this horrible vision of Joanne and Beverly naked on the sheets, passing a cigarette back and forth while Joanne reads aloud from a book of psalms.

Joanne starts talking about a novel she just finished reading which, the way she describes it, sounds like it's heartwarming, comforting and uplifting enough to make you puke right all over the page while you're trying to read the thing.

I butt back in by talking about the novel I'm reading. I happen to be in the middle of another one by the same author. I found out Beatrice had a whole stack of them on a bookshelf in the dining room. When I read aloud to her, Beatrice seems to like the stories a lot too.

"Robert Nathan?" Beverly says, excited. "Oh, he's wonderful. He wrote such beautiful poetry as well. Have you read any of it?"

I say no, but I'd sure like to. Joanne leaves the table to go help Deidre, who's dropped her glasses on the floor and is having trouble finding them. Beverly says she'll bring me a book of this guy's poems next time.

"I might not be here for the next time," I say. "How about we have dinner on Saturday. You could give it to me then."

Beverly's head moves back slightly. Her eyebrows go down a little. It's like out of nowhere I said something in Swahili. I'm nervous enough—it's possible I used a Spanish word.

"We could just meet somewhere," I say, hopefully. "Just so I could borrow those poems."

Beverly draws her chin in and down so the double one bulges, adorable. The whole area around her sweet pink little mouth seems troubled as she studies the paper bouquet in her hands. "Well," she says.

"Or I could pick you up," I say. "Or we can just forget about it. It's no big deal."

"Oh, no," she says. "I'd like to. I'm just thinking. On Saturday nights I usually volunteer at the church bingo. But I could probably get someone to fill in for me. I'm just trying to think who."

Oh, boy. Wow. I can't even believe I did that. I'm stoked. I haven't been this excited in ages. I can't even remember the last time I had a date. If that's what this is. I mean, I don't even know. When is it officially a date and not just meeting a friend for dinner? I don't care. Whatever it is, it feels great. All the way home—listening, as usual, to the swing station—I bounce up and down on the seat while I'm driving. I sing along to lyrics I've never heard before. Beatrice chuckles at me. But I see now why old people like this music; it's honestly happy. It's not like the fake happy, fake sad or fake mad you usually get when you turn on the radio nowadays.

There's a truck that belongs to a land surveying company parked on the side of the road right by the end of the driveway to the farm. One guy is in the middle of the road with a transit on a tripod, looking through it at his rodman further down the road. I roll the window further down as I pull up next to the guy at the transit. He's a pleasant enough looking guy with a dark beard, a belly, pouches under each eye and one in his right cheek.

"You guys are working kinda late," I say.

"Workin' for the man," he says. He spits a brown stream that spatters on the road.

"Which property you surveying?"

"That there one I thought you were about to drive onto," he says, pointing at the farm.

"Why?"

"Gettin' ready to sell it," he says, looking at me curiously now. Maylene, I think. He doesn't know it, but he's working for the woman.

"Well, do you know who's gonna buy it?" I ask.

He turns his head aside to spit again. Only a little of the tobacco juice goes into his beard. "Duke Weeks," he says.

"Dick Weeds? You gotta be shittin' me."

He almost smiles. "Nope. Wish I was. It's nothin' but a goddamn real estate feedin' frenzy around here anymore. They wanna put an office park here." He nods at the piece of land where the only good shit of my entire shitty life ever happened. Mother *fucker*! I can't believe it. I can't say anything more to the surveyor besides thanks. I turn around in the driveway and go back down the road the way we came.

"We're not going home?" Beatrice asks, politely.

"We're going to pay Maylene a little visit," I say.

"Oh, good heavens." Beatrice gets uneasy right away. "That really is the last banana," she says.

It takes almost an hour to get way the hell up to where Maylene lives, so I have plenty of time to think, which in this case means get more pissed off. Never underestimate a ninny. When it comes right down to it, it's the ninnies who run this world. All behind the scenes. And they're at least half the reason it's so fucked up.

Office park. I love these quaint little turns of oxymoron. I really, really do. Office park. I mean, it's like prison camp.

Naturally, Maylene lives in one of these new subdivisions with no trees and the cookie-cutter houses standing around looking naked and humiliated by their ugly shapes. So when I get out and slam the car door, it sounds like a bomb going off and echoes all around me. Maylene's at the end of the cul-de-sac and I had to park on the street a couple doors down because there are all these stupid new cars and SUVs in her driveway and along the curb. Walking toward her house, I forget to put the car keys in my pocket right away. Actually, with the key ring in my fist, three of the keys stick out from between my knuckles. So while they're in my hand they seem to run themselves along the shiny new paint jobs of several of the cars and trucks as I walk along, leaving long white scratches like three-fingered claw marks down their sides.

When I open the door, this pudgy guy in a suit, with a tumbler and a cocktail napkin in his hand, is talking to some dumb, aging bottle-blond and he's right exactly in my fucking way. I don't even push him that hard, but when his back hits the wall, he goes, "Oof," and spills his drink all over himself.

I find Maylene in the kitchen. The way she looks at me, you'd think I was the devil she's been making her deals with. "So, you want to explain why you're putting your own mother, and me, out on the street?" I ask.

The Heart of It All

I'm trying to be polite. But a bunch of people, mostly women who dress as weird as Maylene does, sort of drift back from the island counter they were all gathered around. Some go into the other room. Among other things on the counter, there's a big platter with carrot sticks, broccoli, cubes of cheese and ham, and a bowl of dip in the middle of it.

"I don't know what you're talking about," Maylene says. "I'm not putting anyone ou—"

I grab one end of the platter and flip it upside down onto the floor. Pieces of cheese and broccoli go bouncing off the cabinets. "Answer the *fuck*ing question," I say.

I get checked from the side, and I'd go right onto the floor with the chopped ham except instead I bounce off another body and before I know it these two big guys have me by the arms and they're dragging me backwards. So. Mafia Maylene's even got her own goon squad now. I kick my feet like a crazy dangling puppet. I've been given the bum's rush before, but never in the house of one of my own relatives. When they get me to the door, Maylene catches up and says, Don't, don't, he's my nephew, it's OK. And they stop moving but keep a tight hold of my arms. The one guy's fingers are digging right into my biceps. Maylene says she'd like to talk to me in private if I'll behave myself. So I say I will. The goons let me go and Maylene closes the two of us in this room that could be a guest room, den or whatever. These places have all these useless empty rooms stuck around in them.

"Now look," Maylene says. I look. She's got so much makeup on you'd mistake her for one of those people selling God or jewelry on TV. "I understand that you're concerned about my mother."

"My grandmother," I say.

"But I've made arrangements for her to move into an assisted living facility—one that specializes in Alzheimer's care, you'll be happy to know—in a week."

"So how much they giving you?" I ask.

"Please?"

"I said how much are they giving you to sell your own mom down the river so they can turn our farm into some office hell? I just met the surveyors."

"I'm not discussing my personal business affairs with you."

"You know it's my business too—Jesus Christ—I'm the one who takes care of her. You think I'm going to let you do this?"

"There's nothing you can do, John. She's signed all the papers. I got her evaluated. I have power of attorney and I'm also her legal guardian. The farm is mine now. It's up to me."

I feel my whole body getting tight. If I thought it might help, with one good shot I'd bust Maylene's jaw then get the fuck out of here. I look around this dumb room with vacuum cleaner tracks on the rug.

"Why don't you have Beatrice move in here," I say. "It's not like you don't have the space. You don't need to lock her up in one of those stupid places. How would you like it if Sheila did that to you?"

Maylene's lipstick goes up in a smile. "No, I couldn't have her here. I really don't think that would fit with my lifestyle."

"You don't have a lifestyle," I say. "What you have is a bunch of bullshit." I sweep my arm around to indicate everything from her house to her moral bankruptcy.

Maylene's face chills into its old severity. "Now you listen to me," she says. "I don't know what you've been up to for the last five years," and her eyes bulge and she sticks her chin out at me, which lets me know she talked to Sheila about it, "but you just show up here, thinking you know more than anyone else about right and wrong and how you think everyone else should live. Well, you better start worrying about yourself, buster, because you're going to have to find a place to live in about a month."

I don't know what to say. Or I do, but it would just be a bunch of cuss words at a real high volume. Maylene sighs heavily and shakes her head.

"Look, I'm sorry you had to find out about the farm that way. I was going to tell you this week. But really, you shouldn't be so surprised about this." Then she tells me I look overtired and I ought to go home and try and get some rest. A lot of those people out there are clients of hers and she's got to get back to them. She even rubs my shoulder quick, with a hand and wrist all covered with stones and metals, before she opens the door and tells me she'll call me later. I guess she cares about me in her own way.

No she doesn't. What the hell am I saying?

"Still, nothing you said makes it right, what you're doing," I say, before she can shut the front door on me. "It's just not right."

I go out to the car, but Beatrice isn't in it. I have to go back in Maylene's house and get Beatrice out of this conversation she's having with somebody about Stanley.

Get some rest. Okay, sure. I pace around all night, even smoke a joint—just medical marijuana, for insomnia—and can't get to sleep till around four. I wake up a couple hours later and lie there staring at the trees on my wall, the stars on my ceiling, trying to see if I can tell by how I feel now if it's going to be one of those days where by noon I say to Carlos I should have stayed in bed. Because if that's the case, I'll nip that problem at the bud by just staying put. It's not long before I realize if I stay here, I'm just going to be staring pissed-off at the ceiling for a few hours, so I get up and go. At least it's Friday.

No amigos today. Not even Carlos is here, nobody. I have to go with Terry and Joe. Ryan tells us to take the Bobcat trailer but not the Bobcat. We're going to be picking up a present a customer is giving him for doing such a good job at the shopping center he owns, which Terry's crew landscaped. It turns out to be this tiny old red sports car that doesn't run anymore. Ryan follows us in his truck out to the guy's house, which we're going to work at today. I don't know why Ryan has to come along.

Except that he doesn't trust us to do it right. Like we're too dumb to push a car, I guess.

"I'd give you guys a hand, but I got a bad back," Ryan says, while Joe and I are huffing and puffing behind the rear bumper. "Careful now, Terry. Careful!" he yells.

Terry's in the driver's seat of the little car, with the door open so he can have one hand on the steering wheel and guide the car along. It seems to me he's being careful. Once we have it on the trailer, and I'm hooking up the chains to hold it in place, Ryan says, "She's a beauty, ain't she guys? Huh?" We all sort of mumble what amounts to, Yes master. Ryan rubs his hand slowly over the curved rear of the car in a way that definitely strikes me as perverted. Joe has to stand there with the strap he's going to put across it and wait for Ryan to finish. This is like some moronic industrial abduction. Ryan finally steps back.

"Alfa Romeo," he says, proud. "You know this here car is an Eye-talian?" he asks me. "Sure has an esoteric look to it, don't it? Eh, buddy?"

Yeah, great, like what the hell do we care? Ryan tells us when we go back to the shop to leave it just like this on the trailer in the pit, but make sure and put a tarp over it. He'll pick it up tomorrow morning.

"Oh, shoot," Ryan says, looking at his fancy watch all the sudden. "I got a golf date in less than an hour. Okay, you guys have a good one," he says, heading for his truck. "Enjoy the holiday. And be sure and take good care of my new baby."

I spend most of the day lighting a fire in my lower back while I prune all these hedges. You have to thin-prune them to get out some of the old branches so sunlight can penetrate the plant and then it grows fuller and healthy. You cut down low and at the V where the branch splits. If you just shear off the top now and then, you wind up with a plant that has only a really vulnerable shell of growth around the outside of it. I don't know why I bother even doing my job right. While I work, I wonder if the sports car is part of some crooked business deal. Then I remember I forgot to ask Ryan what the hell is going on with my paychecks.

On our way back to the shop at the end of the day, we pick up a couple more six packs than usual because we know for sure Ryan won't be around. Nobody can believe it's Labor Day already, or so they keep saying. I believe it.

We're all sitting around the pit with open beers, staring at Ryan's new sports car, when Terry says, "You know the only reason that motherfucker came in today was to watch us load up this stupid piece a shit."

"He ain't never gonna be able to find parts for this thing nowheres," says Joe.

"That ain't my point," Terry says.

We see Jim-dandy's truck come in and park over in the warehouse. Terry's truck is still hooked up to the trailer here. We have the beer in his truck to keep it out of the sun. It's still hot as hell out. The pit is like a stinky-ass sauna with piles of shit in it. Jim and Freddie come over to join us.

"Where are the amigos today anyway?" I ask.

"How I heard," Terry says, "Rodriguez ain't been paying them so they're having a strike, kind of."

"How do we know it's not Ryan who's doing all the not paying?" I say. "I mean, maybe Rodriguez doesn't have anything to pay them with."

Joe opens a fresh bottle of beer and flicks the cap at the sports car. "I still ain't been able to get the money from my last check," he says.

Terry climbs up on the trailer and gets in the driver's seat of the little red car. "How do I look in this motherfucker?" he asks.

"You look like a little kid at an amusement park," I say, and flick a bottle cap at him through the open window.

Terry finds a pen on the dashboard and throws it at me, but it hits Joe, who picks up a pebble and throws it at Terry, but hits the door of the car instead.

"Um, you guys I think better be more careful," says Jim.

"Why? You gonna rat on us, motherfucker?" Terry gets out of the car and slams the door, hard.

"I'm just saying Ryan is real concerned about this car. He's been talking about it for weeks."

"To you he's been talking about it," Terry says. "Today when we had to push the fuckin' thing up onto the trailer was the first we heard about it. How'd you know about it? Pillow talk, you and Ryan?"

"I wouldn't be so disrespectful," Jim says.

Terry jumps down from the trailer and gets right in Jim's face. "I'll do what the fuck I want here motherfucker. You got that?"

I open another beer to enjoy while I watch Terry, with his big Irish fists, pound the living shit out of Jim. But Jim's not going for it.

 Terry leans forward to yell a few inches from Jim's face. "I said you understand that, you fuck?"

Jim turns his face like he's suddenly interested in the pile of creek rock over in the corner of the pit. "All right," he says. "Have it your way."

"Damn straight I'll have it my way you piece a shit." Terry goes and gets another beer and flicks the cap, which bounces off the headlight of the sports car.

Jim finishes his beer quietly, puts the empty back in the cardboard container and leaves without saying anything more.

"Damn, Terry," Freddie says. "I think I seen Jim's life flash in front of my eyes just now."

"I'm so sick of that candy ass going around here like him and Ryan is partners," Terry says. "And he only just started workin' here." He guzzles his beer and cracks another one.

"Well, you know Ryan told me I should think of this as my own company too," I say. "I guess he gave Jim the same advice and he really took it to heart."

The Heart of It All

Terry starts flicking pebbles that ping off the hubcap and bumper of the car. "He said he ain't payin' us for Labor Day this year."

"He didn't pay us for the Fourth of July neither," Freddie says. "He told me he's not payin' for no holidays no more."

I start throwing pebbles at the car too. So does Joe. Actually, some of the ones Joe's throwing are bigger than pebbles.

"Looks to me like he just ain't payin' us no more, period," says Joe. "Every time I ask him about my check, he says there's some problem with the bank and he's trying to get it sorted out."

We all keep sinking beers and chucking stones. We get to talking about this and that. Pretty soon there're some little marks in the door of the car. We're looking at these up close, Joe and I—he says it looks to him like storm damage and I say, I got to agree with you there—when Terry comes over, all the muscles bulging out of his freckled forearms, and slams a big chunk of concrete against the rear fender, knocking it half off.

Now none of us is exactly sober, but we all have to agree it looks to us like this sports car Ryan bought wasn't quite in mint condition, now was it? No, if you really take a look at it up close, you can tell it was mixed up in a little fender-bender somewhere along the line. At some earlier point in time.

But, Freddie points out, it has yet to be christened. Joe says, What do you mean? It's like baptizing the thing, I say. Yeah, Freddie says, like they do to a new boat before its first voyage. And wouldn't Ryan probably want us to take care of that for him in case he forgets? So Freddie is the first to smash an empty beer bottle on the hood, but it turns out to be a popular method of disposing of all our empties, so he's not the last.

Then I get an idea. It seems like it's probably just about the best idea I ever had in my whole life. I climb up onto Terry's truck, get a mattock and yell at the other guys to clear the way. Then I yell, "Kawabunga!" leap off the open tailgate, land on the hood of the car and bring the mattock down into it too. It goes in with a cachunk and I yank it out of the hole it made, bringing up a little curl of red metal.

Instantly, I'm like the first man who discovered what he could do if he rubbed two sticks together. The spud bar, ax, spades, shovels all come out of the tool rack and we all go to work on the Alfa Romeo. You would have thought we'd all forgotten we already punched the clock a couple of hours ago. We work with determination and a sense of purpose that is rare among landscapers. The front and back windshields are the first things to go. Then Joe jumps up and down on the roof like he's on a trampoline. I mostly use the mattock, swinging it like I'm trying to hit a home run, and go down the driver's side aiming for a Swiss cheese kind of look even though the car is Italian.

Car-tharsis, is what I'd have to call this. We're all just trying to regulate our own internal combustion here. By the time we're done, the roof is caved in so far the Alfa Romeo looks like a convertible somebody drove through a mine field.

"Okay," Terry says, panting. He drops the spud bar down into the rack on his truck with a clank. "Now don't forget to put a tarp over this baby. We don't want nobody to come by and see it. It could get stolen. Ryan sure would be pissed."

"That's right," Freddie says. "This here's a real bad neighborhood."

"There's all kinds of crazy bastards around here," Joe says. "No telling what they'll get up to."

Then we all bolt.

10

The next day I'm sitting around with Beatrice wondering, so now what? Because I wasn't there long enough to collect unemployment and I don't think Ryan's going to be a very good reference when I apply someplace else, and I have to have a steady job if I'm going to be out of here in a month and dealing with a landlord. I'll probably have to crash with Gary for a while.

And Carla calls. Carla? Yeah, Carla. She'd like to know if I want to come over for dinner tonight. Oh sure, I think, I'll bring the salt. You and Brad can take turns rubbing it in my wounds. She gives me directions and I pretend I need them. Then I hang up the phone and spend the rest of the afternoon pacing around saying, Shit, shit, shit. I'm even making Beatrice nervous. She keeps going, What? What? And, of course, What time is it?

It's now. It's happening. I meant to drive right on past it and go somewhere else. Anywhere. But I go past the clear-cut, pesticide-contaminated golf course, up the ridge, between the brick posts with cement balls on them and past the stone wall that lets you know you're entering Fox Chase Manor. I got here twenty minutes before I'm supposed to be here, where I'm not supposed to be at all. What the hell am I doing?

Carla opens the door, holding a potato masher in her hand like a scepter. She says to come on in. Brad's still out running a few errands. She gives me a beer. Which is my fourth; I wasn't about to come over here stone-cold sober. Carla goes back to making dinner, talking to me over her shoulder like this is okay to do, natural, like I drop by all the time.

But Carla doesn't belong in this place. The house is big and real open with hardly any walls in a lot of the rooms downstairs. I go over to the window in the living area while Carla's talking to me, and look down at the view of the golf course in the twilight. It must have been a fun landscaping job, actually. They got to put in all kinds of hills, knolls, sand traps, puddle ponds and even one hill that drops off like a little cliff on the other side. But when you think of all the water, pipes, machinery and chemicals that go into the constant maintenance of this little topographical fantasyland made for rich people to whack-off—I mean hit—their balls on, it starts to make you queasy.

I look at Carla's back while she's chopping something. You can see the shape of her shoulder blades through her black shirt. The poor thing. She's putting on a good front, but this must be killing her, being trapped in this dumb house, and now with me here she must be aching for all the fun, freewheeling times we had together. What she needs, I realize, is for me to rescue her. I see now that was the whole problem. I wasn't ever strong enough to just sweep her off her feet and carry her into the sunset. Carla bends down and opens the oven to check on what smells like chicken. Is she trying to make a point? "Look how I have to live because you were too chicken to take me away with you." In spite of all our talks about how we were going to escape Ohio, in spite of how we always made fun of the women who came into the bookstore who'd bleached themselves anonymous, Carla ended up having to dye her hair red and settle for the same pampered, suburban death sentence.

When she's in the middle of talking about something else, I say, kind of loud, "Carla." And she looks up, her dark eyes wide. She's expecting something. She knew I'd finally do it, whatever it is I feel I'm about to do.

The Heart of It All

But the feeling is empty pain in my chest. The time between us is worse than distance. There's the sound like someone pounding a little rubber mallet down the hall and before I can say anything else, this miniature barefooted human being runs into the kitchen, going, "Mommy, Mommy." It stops when it sees me. Then, walking real slow over to Carla, it keeps its eyes on me, ready in case I spring suddenly with my claws and fangs out. Once it's got Carla's pants in its fist, the little person says, "Mommy, who's that man?"

Carla leads him over and introduces me to Jeremy. "Why don't you show John your dinosaurs for a couple of minutes while I finish getting dinner ready?" she says.

"Okay," Jeremy says, like she just told him he has to go electrocute himself.

I follow Jeremy into a room that's so full of toys you can barely walk. He shows me all these plastic dinosaurs and in no time we're making them roar at each other on the rug, chase each other around, and of course kill each other. Generally, the longest, most violent death, with the grossest noises and groans of pain, is the type that makes Jeremy the happiest. He's got Carla's hair and eyes. The whole time we're playing, I keep thinking, this should have been my son.

Jeremy asks if I want to see where he hides his jelly beans. I say sure and he gets out this little box from behind some books on the bookshelf. I notice they only have two Pixies books in here. We start eating the jelly beans Jeremy gives out one at a time like they're valuables.

"They all have different flavors," he reminds me. With his tiny fingers he fishes out a red one and puts it in my hand. "That one tastes red," he says.

"And the green ones make you horny," I say.

He asks, What's horny? And I wonder, should I tell him? "You see kid, in a few years this agony is going to take hold of your body and control about three quarters of the shit you do for the rest of your life."

But why ruin the surprise?

"Well," I say, "it's a feeling you get when you're like really, really happy and it makes you so excited you do weird things."

"Like what?" he wants to know.

"Like, you start jumping up and down," I say.

He says that's really neat and he goes through his box of jelly beans, popping all the green ones in his mouth. Then damned if he doesn't start jumping up and down. I swear, the whole human race is a bunch of drug addicts just waiting to happen.

Through the window, I see the SUV pull in the driveway. So, it's his. Somehow, I don't want them talking about me in the kitchen while I'm in here playing dinosaurs and eating jelly beans. So I suggest to Jeremy we go see how dinner is coming along. I need another beer anyway if I'm going to survive all this.

"Hey, how's it going," Brad says, shaking my hand. No way can he really be happy to see me. I just stare at him. I want to say, So, how'd you imagine you were actually going to get away with this? He puts more gel in his hair than ever and he stinks from some cologne that somehow matches his heartland-hipster clothes.

"Let me get you another of those," he says, when he notices the empty bottle in my hand.

I simply can't believe this. I mean, he looks and acts like some kind of comedy skit: Suburban Elvis. I watch this freak of nature get me a beer out of the fridge and then Carla tells the thing to finish making the salad. When is she going to pull me aside and make a joke about this guy? He's exactly the kind of person we always hated and made fun of. And I can't look at him. Or I can. But every time I do, I think, So this is the guy who's fucking my wife.

Jeremy comes into the kitchen and starts jumping up and down. "Look Mom," he says. "Look how horny I am."

There's a stereo they keep hidden in a big wooden cabinet. They put some music on that's not bad, but it's like you're always waiting for it to speed up, or somebody to start screaming. Anything. It's the stuff they'd probably play if there were a Carington Valley for young people. I guess Carla's gotten a long ways from the Ramones.

This complete lack of reality settles over the whole scene. I feel like I wandered onto a stage where actors are performing some play I never heard of. I say these lines I hope will fit in with the gist of things. There's a baby on the counter in a plastic bucket you can strap into the car or just carry around. Brad must have brought it in. He and Carla ask me questions about Beatrice and about my job. I answer.

Carla leaves the room with the baby-in-a-bucket and Jeremy pulls Brad by the hand out into the other room to show him a drawing he did. I'm left alone on stage. The keys to the SUV are on the counter. I pick them up to look at them and then, because it seems to be the right thing, or just because I can, or because it feels like the audience expects me to, I slip them in my pocket. You know, people just leave shit lying around.

Brad comes back in, all smiles. I consider beating the crap out of him right quick and putting him in the trunk of my car to kill later so that Carla and I can have dinner alone and get things sorted out between us.

"Anybody ever slice one through the living room window?" I ask, holding my beer up in the direction of the view.

He chuckles. No, no, it'd have to be a pretty long shot.

"So you're lawyering now?" I say, in a way I try to make sound more like "loitering."

"Yup," he says, opening a beer for himself. "A few buddies and I just started our own practice."

"It's still just practice though, huh. Like not for real?" Then I ask him what you call a thousand dead lawyers.

"A good start," he says. "I've heard them all." He grins and takes a swig of beer. I think we both know what we're thinking at this point. I mean, that grin of his is like, "Me good hunter. Me take Carla."

I wonder if you punched the end of a beer bottle while somebody was drinking from it, if you hit it hard enough, you could drive the thing right up into their brain and kill them. But I'd settle for smashing all Brad's teeth out and watching him stagger around the room with the bottle stuck halfway down his throat and blood streaming down his neck.

"Is the funny man staying for dinner?" I hear Jeremy asking Carla from the other room, their voices approaching the kitchen. She tells him yes, the funny man is staying for dinner. "Is he going to stay overnight?" he asks. Carla says probably not.

This appears to be some kind of end-of-the-summer Thanksgiving special in the dining room, with roast chicken, mashed potatoes and gravy and whatnot. When I put the first bite in my mouth, I remember where I'm supposed to be. An hour ago. I picture Beverly, smelling of an extra hint of that awful cheap perfume I love, standing outside the restaurant where I told her we'd meet, with a book of poems in one hand, checking the thin watch on her plump wrist. Probably making an excuse for me in her mind: "Something must have happened to Beatrice. He's probably taking her to the hospital. I should go call and make sure they're both okay."

I am the worst kind of fuck-up. I really ought to just drop dead already. I don't deserve to have dinner with a woman like Beverly in the first place, much less lay a finger on her. No, what I deserve is to sit here with my ex-girlfriend and her dork husband, eating my humble pie. But I don't have an appetite now. Can't remember the last square meal I had, but still I can't eat any more. The last bite of chicken I took is turning into a piece of damp plaster in my mouth.

Jeremy asks Carla if he can go watch some TV show. Tells me to come and get him when it's time for desert. When he leaves I think I've lost my only ally here. We hardly talk till there's the sound of somebody torturing a cat upstairs and Carla looks at Brad and asks does he mind this time? She just needs the bottle, Carla says, and to be joggled for a minute.

Mr. Efficient gets up, leaves the dining room and I think, man, is he ever whipped! Carla bosses him around like her little servant boy. I'd never ever let that happen to me. In the midst of this terrible sinking feeling I've had since we sat down, I all the sudden feel free. This isn't my life. I could get up and dance on the table, punt the chicken carcass right into the other room. After desert, I'll say I have to hurry up and go, got to catch a flight in the morning. Oh, I didn't mention that? Yeah, can't seem to kick the habit of these singles cruises in the Bahamas. Especially when there are so many hot mamas out there looking for a stud like me!

Like who the hell are you kidding? You'd give your right arm, left leg, both eyes and throw in an ear to be able to live with Carla. You'd lick her boots clean every morning if that's what she wanted, you suffering sack of shit.

Carla puts her fork down after Brad leaves the room and rubs her temples. "Sometimes I can't wait to get back to work," she says.

I don't say anything. I've spread the food around on my plate but not much is gone. We can hear the TV, and after a little bit the baby stops crying.

"So what happened?" I say.

"What?" Carla asks.

"To you."

"I'm not sure what you mean," she says.

Then there's this look on her face that forces me into the spot-lit reality of why I'm here. Carla felt sorry for me. That look—it's pity. Well that's just great. Perfect. That's all I need. I can't stay here another second. I get up abruptly, accidentally knock over my wine glass and say, I gotta go. I'm out of the room, heading for the door before she can say it.

"John," she calls after me, and that's the last thing I hear her say. That's what I really want. All I want is to hear her call my name. I know she'd never come after me.

On the seat of Beatrice's car there's a solitary green jelly bean waiting for me. That kid is going to be all right. Even if his dad is a total fucking prick.

It sure is a good thing they still have these drive-through liquor stores in this state. Sometimes, really, you hardly feel like slowing down, never mind getting out of the car, for another drink. Now, don't get me wrong, I'm no fan of drinking and driving. But if you stay on roads you know well and make sure to put your hand over one eye to keep you from seeing double, usually you're going to be okay. So I drive around till I get myself pretty numb and then go home.

Gary doesn't want to pick me up. Says I sound pretty much wasted and he's still not too happy about the Heighberger house job.

"Lissen," I say, swaying over the phone. "All I need for you to do is drop me off somewhere. You can do this one blind."

It works. Gary makes it clear he wants no info about what I'm going to do when he drops me off just past the Fox Chase Manor gate. I have to walk a little ways. Even if you're shitfaced, it's eerie to be in a quiet, new, plastic neighborhood like this at night; it's kind of like a freshly made ghost town. I get to the house. The only problem now, as I'm wobbling around Carla's driveway, is how do I get in the garage? I walk around the side where there's no light, roll my ankle in a little drainage gully or something and fall down. I get up, and as I start feeling my way along the wood siding of the garage in the dark, my hand hits something metal. A little flap. I lift it up, feel a button, and think, what a weird place for a doorbell. Then a grinding noise breaks the silence, and the garage starts hauling its door up to the ceiling, and from inside, light dawns on the asphalt driveway. I scoot in there, hop in the SUV, back it out, and head on down Fox Chase Trail Road.

And now I see why people like these things. I mean, I'm sitting way up high, almost like I'm in a landscaping truck, but man, I feel invincible.

The Heart of It All

And I know a great place with all kinds of fun terrain to do some four-wheeling. Right nearby. There's chain link fence all around it till I get to a stretch along the road where there's just a wooden rail. But that doesn't stand a chance. I hardly feel anything, and—because the only song I like by Ratt just came on the radio and I turned it full-blast—don't even hear the bump as I plow right through. You could drive one of these things around, knocking people off motorcycles left and right and not even know about it.

Then I'm spinning around, doing donuts on one of the putting greens. Chunks of turf go flying out from under the tires till it's all gone and I just send a nice spray of soil all around me as I go round and round. It's going to be a real challenge to do any more putting on here. That's all right. I hate golf. I hate golfers. I've had enough.

I go off the green, ramp a little hummock and right away get stuck half-in, half-out of a kidney-shaped sand trap. Of all the goddamn crappy, unreliable SUVs. Just when I was thinking I might have to get one of these rigs for myself, it fails the test drive miserably. Then I look down and realize I don't even have it in four-wheel-drive yet.

Now that's more like it! Awesome! I come lurching right out of the sand trap and I'm back in business. Tearing all around. I feel sorry for people who spend all day playing golf. To get around some of these little hills they have to get off their cart, walk over in their goofy pants, pick the right club, and chip a white ball. Whereas I just floor it and go flying over the hill, catch a little air under my tires, and come bouncing back down on the other side.

Great shocks on this thing. Handles great, too. Who'd a thunk that on grass that's cut to a quarter inch, a big old tank like this could turn on a dime and go ripping back across in the other direction? I can't believe I've been pooh-poohing these things all along. I'm having the time of my life in this baby. Taking the little hills like a skier taking moguls.

And look at this now. Other people got the same idea. There are a few pairs of headlights coming across the course. It's just like when you think you found a video game machine you're going to have all to yourself for the next little while. Forget it. Terry's right, there's just too many motherfuckers.

But these motherfuckers are cops! They can't fool me—I can see the flashing lights on the tops of their cars. Cops driving their cruisers around on the golf course in the middle of the night, Jesus Christ! I mean, look at where our tax dollars are going. Not only that, they're terrain hogs. Got to come right over to my area by the ninth hole, or wherever I am, and try and cut me off. Can't they see what the hell I'm behind the wheel of? Well, this bastard, if he can't see, feels it. Because I plow right into the front end of his puny cop car, spin it sideways and keep on going. So long! There are the two behind me now, but there's no way they're going where I'm going. They don't have four-wheel-drive.

I haven't ramped this little rise yet, it's new to me. But now, just as I reach the top of it, I kind of remember maybe seeing this one from the window at Carla's. Right now, if she was to look down from there, she'd see these different pairs of headlights, as they go bouncing over hills, bobbing all around in the darkness below her like little boats being tossed around in a stormy sea. If she knew I was the captain of one of these vessels, would she be worried? I wonder. If I died out here, would she sometimes go out at sunset with an ache in her chest, and pace her back porch like it was a widow's walk and think about my silly lost soul? In my stomach, soon as I launch Brad's craft from the little cliff, there's that loose feeling of all your internal organs floating around inside your rib cage, like you get when your plane drops suddenly in turbulence. It doesn't seem like I'm ever going to hit.

11

So now I'm real popular. All you have to do is act like the biggest freaking asshole you can imagine in this world and everybody wants to visit you and talk to you. Carla, Brad, Jeremy and Ann, the bucket baby, came in yesterday morning.

The air bag didn't open up, so I got a concussion, four busted ribs and a cracked kneecap. They tell me I'm very lucky. And I'm not in nearly as deep a shit as I thought. Turns out Brad is friends with the son of the guy who owns the golf course and he even knows the judge who's jurisdiction this falls under. Course Brad and Carla aren't going to press charges. They told the cops they'd loaned me the SUV. I told Brad maybe he could help me try and sue the company that makes the crummy SUVs, since their air bag didn't open. But I could tell by the look on his face I was pushing it. It was too nice of them all to come in here like that anyway. Jeremy was real serious and concerned, and when he taped up to the wall by my bed the dinosaur drawings he'd made for me, I wanted to cry. I pretended I was a lot more out-of-it from the painkillers than I really was so they'd hurry up and leave.

One of the things they told me before they left was not to worry, everybody had plenty of insurance. But that's not true; I don't have any insurance. When Sheila, Maylene and Beatrice came in today, their second visit, Maylene said she'd take care of it—meaning the hospital bill—she felt so bad. But she had a look on her face like she'd been shopping and got a bargain. Beatrice put her soft, wrinkled hand on my forehead, just under the bandage. She left it there for a full minute while she looked into my eyes like she was going into a trance. "You're going to be fine," she said, at last, and removed her hand.

A few hours later Terry, Joe and Freddie come in. They all look different. I've never seen any of them cleaned up before and wearing clothes besides the green RR t-shirts. First thing Joe wants to know is if there are any hot nurses.

Terry makes his voice nasally to mimic Ryan, and says, "So, you enjoying your holiday?"

"God damn, dawg," Freddie says. "You got your ass *all* busted up."

"So you guys all going out job hunting tomorrow?" I ask.

"You ain't never gonna believe this dude," Terry says. "But Ryan called me on Saturday and he's got no idea we done it."

"How?"

Terry gets out a cigarette, then remembers where he is and sticks it behind his ear. "Well, we all left in such a hurry the other night we must of left the gate to the pit unlocked. Somebody stole the chain and the padlock that night I guess because Ryan said when he come by the next morning they was gone, and the gate was standing wide open. So he figures some kids in the neighborhood broke in and when they couldn't get the car started, decided they'd beat the shit out of it."

"Like when anything bad goes down in this city," Freddie says. "We just gonna let the blame fall on the niggas."

After they leave, I lie there, looking out the window. From up here, you can see across the industrial cesspool of a valley they call Spring Grove. I can hear the screech of trains on the rusted tracks down there. I guess that's what that noise is. The angle of the sunlight already has that nostalgic slant to it that it gets in the fall. Before you know it, the leaves will be changing. Here in the Nasty they don't turn color so much as just get kind of sickly looking and then fall off their branches.

I know I can't stay here. Not now. They're going to hit me with some fines, but you can always work out some low monthly payment plan if you're poor enough. I'll still have money to get out of town. I just don't know where to go yet.

Maylene said I can stay at the farmhouse for a while since she's put the brakes on the sale for now. But she already abducted Beatrice and it's way too quiet in the house. The cot I set up in the living room I didn't think would end up being for me, but what with this brace on my leg and the crutches, it's much less of a pain in the ass to just sleep down here.

But today I'm going upstairs anyway. Part of the deal is I'm supposed to help out by starting to box up some of the books and other stuff to get it ready to move out. I decided I'm going to take it from the top, even though Maylene said I only have to do the first floor. So I hobble all the way up to the attic.

After a little while it's clear to me I'm not doing any packing today— it's more like browsing. I find this box that's got a bunch of old dirt-stained baseballs, a few baseball gloves and other stuff. I pull out a long, rectangular, framed black and white photo of a bunch of kids in matching t-shirts, lined up in front of a sign that says "Camp Wanatchee." You can see from their haircuts that it's about 1950. There's my skinny little dad, smiling in the sunshine with everybody else, his arms folded across his chest so he can try and make his chicken-wing biceps look bigger. If you look at this and the old baseball glove stained dark brown in the middle where his twelve-year-old hand caught baseballs, you can't even imagine that he would grow up to be the kind of guy who, one drunken night, decides to haul off and deck his own twelve-year-old. Not that I didn't probably deserve it. But still it's sad because he was just this grown-up skinny little kid who didn't know what he was doing. His dad was an asshole before him. If there's one thing this asshole, I mean me, is determined to not be, it's an asshole dad.

The leather in the middle of the baseball glove is soft and crisscrossed with zillions of tiny little wrinkles like Beatrice's face.

Baseball is such a dumb cowpoke kind of game. I always hated it. I'm not going to pack up anything for Maylene. She can try and handle all this crap herself, or, knowing her, hire somebody else to pack it all up. I'm not the one who wants to destroy this place.

I hear the phone ringing and I drop the baseball glove, stand up quick, twist sideways and my ribs send sharp pains shooting through me to let me know not to do this again. I go gimping down the steep stairs and pick up the phone.

"Stanley?" she says. It's Beatrice. She sounds maybe a tiny bit ticked off.

"Beatrice?" I say.

"Who's this?" she asks.

"It's John," I say. "How're your new digs?"

There's a pause. I can hear a couple other voices in the room wherever she is in the nursing home or whatever you want to call it. "Please, I'd like to speak with my husband," Beatrice says.

"Grandma, you know you can't do that anymore."

"I know what's going on," she says. "I know why I'm here. You can tell him I know what he's up to. He can't fool me—oh!" There's a bang. I think the receiver got dropped on something hard.

"Hello?" It's a young woman's voice.

"Hello," I say.

"I apologize. One of our residents here got hold of the phone."

"That's okay. She's my grandmother."

After I hang up, I know I have to stop putting off the one apology I definitely have to make. I dial the number of the daycare center and Beverly picks up on the first ring. Before I have a chance to really think of something.

"Hello?" she says a second time, after I don't say anything. "Hello?" Her voice is hopeful, friendly. But it won't be when she finds out it's the guy who stood her up. I'm pretty sure it's Virginia I can hear in the background singing, "Life is a cabaret, old chum!"

"Hello? Can I help you?" Beverly tries one last time.

And I hang up. No, you can't help me. I'm beyond that, Bev. Sorry. Might as well leave her alone; let her help the ones she can.

"I'm sorry," I say aloud, to the hung-up old rotary phone sitting on its little mahogany stand in the hall. My voice fades into the yellowing wallpaper around me. "I'm sorry, I'm sorry, I'm sorry!"

"Jeez, John," Ryan says, when I go in to pick up my last check. "Looks like I'm going to have to keep you on the injured list for a while."

"Yeah, for good," I say.

His brain starts squirming around and his eyebrows are like caterpillars in their death throes. He wants to know what I mean. I wonder if you just pressed your finger on Ryan's forehead while he was talking, he'd just shut down, stop mid-sentence with his mouth open and a blank stare on his face.

"I'm moving to Chicago," I say. And then we both stand there for a second staring at each other in shock, because I didn't know that was my plan either till I said it. Then he's shaking my hand, saying, that's great buddy, slapping my shoulder, saying Break a leg, ha, ha, just kidding.

And I see all the sudden he knows. Course he knows. It doesn't take a Ph.D. in psychology to figure out that if you keep ripping people off, eventually they're going to do something. Strike back. Now he's being extra nice because he's scared to death of what the hell else we might do. I could raise my crutch and smack the side of his head with it a couple times and he'd just try and laugh it off.

The envelope he handed me I wave in front of his face. "Now this isn't going to turn out to be made outta rubber, is it Ryan?"

Oh, ha, ha, ha, he says, no, not to worry, he's got everything all squared away now. Then he's practically shoving me out the door of his cruddy little office. And why not? I mean, the season's about over. Next spring will bring another batch of suckers to his door.

Terry's truck pulls up as I'm unlocking the door to Beatrice's car, which I'm not supposed to be driving on account of my knee. The leg's got to stay straight. But I've found I can stick it over on the passenger's side and work the gas and brake with my left foot. It's an automatic.

"Hey hop-along, how's it goin'?" Terry asks, after he gets out of the truck. I tell him okay, and then start elaborating on my brand new plan to move to Chicago, which sounds better the more I talk about it. I'll be in a city I could stand, where at least there's shit to do, plus I won't be so far away I can't visit Beatrice regularly.

Carlos gets out of the truck and comes over, looking like somebody just drained all the blood out of him. You can hardly see the little bump on his thin nose from where the limb came down on him. But he's so damn pale.

"Qué pasa?" I ask.

"Estoy enfermo," he says.

"He forgot his burrito today," Terry says. "I went into a Mickey D's and got a couple burgers for him. Half an hour later, the motherfucker starts puking all over the place. The meat musta been bad or something."

Carlos is looking around, kind of glassy-eyed. "Este país quiere matarme," he says.

I remember how Carla told me one time that most of the native North Americans were killed off by diseases the Europeans brought over. The way we're going to kill off the South and Central Americans is by working them, nickel and diming them and feeding them fast food. When I was in the hospital, I was reading in the paper about how our president is trying to improve our relationship with Mexico. You know the end is near as soon as you hear that. When Carla and I were on the outs, she was constantly talking about "the relationship." She started making noises about her "investment." People mean business. Sooner or later you have to face that.

"Pobrecito," I tell Carlos, and he calls me a pendejo. I explain to him that I'm going away and that night, lying there on the cot in the living room, I wonder if I am or what. I can't get to sleep because I can't stop thinking. I think the main reason people go to work is because you can go there and put your mind to sleep. Without a job and with no place to go, you stare at the ceiling and keep replaying everything, trying to convince yourself you're figuring things out. Maybe I'll just lie here and let them bulldoze the house down with me in it; it seems like a heroic way to go, lying down in protest, without so much as a whimper being crushed by the progress of the rapidly evolving office park people.

Every once in a while somebody's face from the past comes bobbing up to the surface of my consciousness and it takes me a minute to figure out why. There was this guy, Tom, who lived with Gary and me for a while. He and Gary were practically inseparable for a while because they were exact opposites. Tom was real high-energy, zipping all over the place like a pinball. We always said his metabolism was so fast that if he gulped an air bubble the way you do to make yourself burp, a second later he'd fart instead. And he farted an awful lot. He had a thing for farts. He'd go up to people on the street and tell them to pull his finger and he'd fart. We'd be sitting on the couch watching TV and he'd whip out a lighter and flick it by his butt and fart on it to see the flame go higher.

Once, at this parade downtown, he and a couple friends of his from art school took off all their clothes behind a dumpster in an alley, put on ski masks and sneakers, and with nothing else on went running screaming through the middle of the parade. They got a couple cops chasing them but they got away somehow.

Another time we were at this party and Tom took three tabs of acid by accident instead of one. When we realized it, he just kind of laughed and said, Oh well, shit happens, or something like that. And he rode it out just fine. Except for this one kind of upsetting interlude that lasted for about an hour where he was completely convinced that Gary was actually the devil. But we managed to talk him out of it.

Tom was just basically and all-around great guy, is what I'm getting at. The world would be better with more guys like that in it. And at the beginning of the summer, Gary told me Tom was living in Chicago now. So I get his number from Gary and when I call Tom he says, "Yeah dude, come on up here." He talks like a mile a minute. "You can crash at my place. It's not very big, but no problem. You'll love it up here man. I can't stand the Nasty. I don't know how you're doing it." He tells me he's writing and illustrating his own comic books and I wonder how come I never thought of doing that.

One time when I was in Alaska, I called Sheila and she told me she was dating a guy who she wasn't too sure about because he told her he worked as a day trader. Of course I had no idea what she was talking about till she explained it, but my first thought was, man, what an honest person. Because all I know is, we all have to trade our days for something else. Problem is deciding on what's worth trading them for. I think maybe Tom's onto something.

I think about how Sheila said I should maybe dedicate my life to saving the planet or whatever. I don't know. I mean, I read this article in a magazine once about how, chances are, sooner or later, the earth is going to be hit by a giant meteor and every single thing in the whole world that doesn't get killed right away is going to die slowly because of all the smoke that's going to be blocking the sunlight for a long time. And I thought, shit. Here I am having a personal crisis every time I throw away a Styrofoam up. I don't know what the hell you're supposed to do. At the end of the day, what really matters? I can't even think about all this stuff right now.

But I'm still thinking about all this stuff when I see Sheila's car in the parking lot of Beatrice's new home institution. The crutches make me feel like a big pair of scissors slicing its way along. Inside, this place is Carington Valley except nicer, with not even prints but actual paintings on the walls. There are these big polished wooden handrails all along the hallways like in a ballet studio. But no mirrors of course. Wouldn't want the residents scaring the shit out of themselves every few minutes. They'd be like kids screaming, running around in a not-so-fun-house all day long.

There's an old framed photograph of Stanley outside Beatrice's door. His hair is greased back and he's in a jacket and tie, smiling out at you with his mouth open a little like he's about to say he's so pleased to meetcha. It's one of the publicity photos for the Pixies books from way back. Beatrice's name is painted on this ceramic tile on her door, with kind of sloppily painted Pixies dancing around it. I notice some of the other people have whole trophy cases full of memorabilia next to their doors. It's so they know which is their room.

I knock, Maylene opens the door and demands to know what I'm doing here since I'm not supposed to be driving. The annoyance is like static electricity filling the room. Maylene is annoyed because she's here, and Beatrice annoyed for the same reason. But Sheila sits there smiling in the midst of this storm of negative energy and tells me I look much better. Which of course is horseshit.

But as I lower myself into one of the institutional chairs that have high seats so old people don't have to lower themselves too dangerously far down, I notice Beatrice does look better. She doesn't look so tired and disheveled. Her hair is clean and shiny. She even smells nice. Beatrice looks more like the dignified old woman she is, in her gray flannel skirt and white blouse, even though you can see her clothes and shoes have Velcro everywhere instead of buttons and zippers and laces. Still, I guess it's better than her going around with her shoelaces trailing and her blouses buttoned all cockeyed with the saggy skin of her chest showing, like when I let her dress herself.

"Thank goodness you're here," Beatrice says.

I don't know yet if I'm me or my dad.

Beatrice is sitting in one of these higher armchairs too. Sheila and Maylene sit in chairs that were brought over from the farmhouse to make Beatrice feel at home. Maylene's in this bright red getup. She sits down and crosses her legs and sits up too straight like she's on a talk show or whatever. Some people think their relationship with their own fantasies of themselves is more important than their relationships with other people.

"I guess you might as well join us," Maylene says, like I haven't already done it. "But we'll all have to be leaving in a few minutes anyway. Mother has her painting class."

"They just got here," Beatrice says to me. She's been examining the wreck of me since I sat down. It's slowed up the nervous darting her eyes were doing when I first came in. The hand she was using to bunch her skirt up in her fist she raises to her face. She runs her fingertips back and forth over her wrinkled lips as she looks at the crutches I just put on the floor between us.

"We were just discussing Beatrice's new quarters," Maylene says, primly. "Just making small talk."

"They make talk so small you don't even notice it," Beatrice says, smiling at me. She leans forward and runs her hand along the brace that covers most of my leg. She makes a few tisking sounds with her tongue and says, "Oh dear."

As she does this, I notice there's a plastic bracelet around her shriveled wrist and I bend over too, to look at that. It's got her name and the address and phone number of this place on it. A dog collar. Maylene must feel triumph at last.

There's a loud scraping sound as Beatrice, real quick, yanks open one of the Velcro straps on my brace. "Ah," she says. "I see they've got you all tied up with the vellum, too. I honestly don't care for this hotel. Not one bit." She looks into my eyes, real sincere. "I know why he put me in here."

"Mother," Maylene says.

But Beatrice doesn't turn toward her; she just winces, then gets a more determined look. "He's having an affair," she says. "I know how he gets when he's in those moods and the drinking. He's carrying on with some young woman at the house."

"Well, I've been there," I say. "I think I would have noticed if that was going on."

Sheila blows some air through her teeth and shifts around in her chair. Beatrice nods at me, real solemn.

"He even changed the phone number," Beatrice says. "But I looked it up in the history book."

There's a knock on the door and a woman with short black hair peeks in. She says she was coming by to remind Beatrice about her painting class, says she didn't realize Beatrice had company. Maylene says that's all right and gets up. We were just leaving, she says. But I say I'm staying, I'll go to painting class with Beatrice. You can tell by the constipated look on her face, Maylene really doesn't approve of this idea at all and she gets a little salty. After the woman leaves, Maylene scolds Beatrice and me thoroughly and stalks on out the door. Sheila tells me she'll stop by the farm tomorrow afternoon and I don't bother telling her I'm not going to be there by then.

Beatrice and I get down to the arts and crafts room and who's here but Cliff and Mildred. Beatrice is in a good mood now that Maylene's gone.

"It's wonderful to see you," she says to Mildred.

"Why?" says Mildred. She looks more paranoid than ever. Cliff, on the other hand, looks much better rested. While Mildred and Beatrice take their seats around the table with the other folks, Cliff pulls me aside. He asks, and I tell him about my injuries, how I got them falling off the tailgate of one of the landscaping trucks where I work.

"Did you hear about the other night?" he says. I didn't. "One of the residents here, a man, went into the room of the woman who lives right next door to Mildred. He got into bed with her." Cliff swallows and his Adam's apple seems to travel an awful long way down and then back up in his old turkey throat. "The attendants came in when she started screaming. And the man started crying and curled up in the corner. They ended up having to carry him back to his room. He'd thought this other woman was his wife who's been dead for fifteen years."

"Well, I guess the old itch never quite goes away, does it?" I say. Cliff doesn't seem to want to respond to that. He's a little astonished, actually. I think I see what it is about him. He doesn't make me feel guilty so much as just plain bored. He's a gossip.

"I'm just thanking my lucky stars that guy didn't go into Mildred's room," he says. "She would've been upset for a week."

I doubt she'd remember it that long, but I don't say anything except that I want to see what Beatrice is up to. I pull up a chair between Beatrice and this other woman who hasn't started painting on her piece of paper yet. She just stares at it and nods up and down. She keeps murmuring, "Possum, possum. Possum and arpeggio for going juice pine."

Beatrice smiles warmly at me as I ease myself down. On accident, I bump a guy's foot under the table with my bum leg and he immediately pushes back from the table, gets down on his hands and knees and is going to start crawling under the table when an attendant catches up with him.

The staff here doesn't seem like the type at Carington Valley that were just doing their jobs as chores that had to get done between trips to the all-you-can-eat roadside buffets. These people here actually give a shit. The woman with the short black hair comes over to show her interest in Beatrice's confused swirls of color that are all over her piece of paper and on the butcher paper around it that the table is covered by. At first I want to tell this lady she doesn't have to suggest Beatrice use more yellow in her painting because, after all, Beatrice is a famous children's book illustrator goddamnit, so why don't you just buzz off! But what would that do except prove I'm a crazy ass? Because this lady is just being nice and Beatrice is obviously happy here. Humming to herself while she dabs and smears the paint around with her brush. I should have gotten her to try this back at the house.

After we leave and are heading back down the hall toward her room, Beatrice stops walking all the sudden. "I know," she says.

"What?" I say.

"Let's go to the snooze-a-little room." She turns around and starts going back the other way. "It's around here somewhere," she says.

There's a little plaque that says "Snoezelen Room," on the wall by the door. Everywhere in the whole facility there are labels and usually pictures, too. Like on the door to the bathroom in the hall there's a picture of a toilet.

There are a couple other people sitting in armchairs in this psychedelic room Beatrice leads me into. The lighting is dim. In the center of the room are these big glass tubes of water with lights shining up through them and air bubbles constantly rising up. Big lava lamps, more or less. One whole wall is taken up by this shifting kaleidoscope of colors being projected onto it from a hole in the opposite wall. The music coming in is the kind of floaty stuff they play when you're visiting the aquarium.

An old woman holding a large purse on her lap glares at us when we come in, but her face relaxes again when we sit down.

"Isn't this nice?" Beatrice asks me.

I have to admit I like it. Beatrice watches the colors expanding, contracting, fading in and out of each other on the wall. She shrugs her itty bitty shoulders and sighs. "We can stay here until dinner time," she says. She waves to an old guy sitting across the room from us and he gets a vague look of recognition on his face, smiles and waves back. Then Beatrice turns and passes the smile to me, her round little cheeks bunching up out of the wrinkles. Here she is, a Pixie in her tree house with all these little wonders around her. She reaches over and pats my wrist.

"So. Tell me all about it," she says.

"Well," I say, "I guess I'm going to be moving on again."

She gives my wrist a brisk rubbing then puts her hand back in her lap. Behind her, the brightly lit bubbles in one of the tubes keep rising up to the ceiling. "You never could stay put," she says.

"You mean me, John?" I say.

"You, John," she says. "The day you were born, bouncing around like a Mexican jumping frog. Getting into everything. You were my dream come true."

I pick her little hand back up off her lap. "I love you," I say.

The plastic bracelet slips back down her wrist as she puts her other hand on top of mine. "Of course," she says.

The only time the Pixies ever use modern transportation is in an episode in one of the books where they borrow somebody's car to go for a joy ride that naturally ends in disaster. The rest of the time they're just running around on foot or borrowing somebody's horse or bicycle or, in the one where they go to the North Pole, they use skis and snow shoes.

After I buy my bus ticket at the window, the only place to sit in the whole terminal is one of these plastic chairs that has a TV attached to it that you can pay to watch. At least I don't have to take a plane and sit in the airport where you have to hear and see a TV whether you like it or not. I know it's a great democratic deal and everything, because otherwise we might forget what to buy, but where the hell was I when they put this question on the ballot and you could vote on if we should all be forced to watch TV even when we're pumping gas or whatever.

So anyway I sit down and watch the TV till I run out of quarters. But I still have an hour left before my bus comes, so I get a sketch pad out of my pack. In the back of the pad I have one of Beatrice's new paintings. She insisted I take with me. It looks like a Jackson Pollock. But wherever I end up, I'm going to hang it on my wall.

I get out a pencil and start trying to draw just some of the empty seats and the buses outside the terminal window. I doodle. I make some cartoons. I decide I don't have to draw exactly what Beatrice drew. I don't know what I'm going to do. Right now, I'm just drawing stuff. That's all. I'll figure something out. The Pixies always survive to go on to the next adventure. We can get away with anything.